High Five!

[signature]

Pork Buns and High-Fives

by Norma Slavit

Illustrated by J L Tolley

Pork Buns and High-Fives

ISBN: 978-0-578-22494-7
Library of Congress: TX 8-819-690

Published by Norma Slavit, San Jose, California 95129.
Printed in the United States of America.

In the event Norma Slavit is not available, her son, Joel Slavit, of San Carlos, California 94070, will act in her behalf for any business pertaining to this book.

Illustrator: Jude Tolley, San Jose, California 95131.

Pictures of the photographs on the wall at Chef Chu's Restaurant on page 56 and 57 and photographs on page 117 of the outside of Chef Chu's taken by Luanna K. Leisure, Campbell, California 95008.

Family photographs on page 120 and 121 provided by Larry Chu, Los Altos California 94022.

Permission has been granted by Chef Chu to reprint his pork bun recipe on page 118.

To order additional books go to: **http://www.LuLu.com, Amazon.com or Barnes&Noble.com**
Email: nslavit@hotmail.com

Table of Contents

Table of Contents

Chapter

Book Reviews

This is a wonderful, coming-of-age, true story of an Asian boy growing up in Silicon Valley. The author provides an interesting example about feeling or being different. The story shares a powerful theme of overcoming these feelings. It is easily relatable because, at some point, we all feel this way, in some shape or form.

Receiving love, support and encouragement from his mother, Larry is able to rise above his personal challenges.

Scott Riches
President, Pinewood School
Los Altos, California

This is a most inspiring story — full of parental wisdom, direction and love. Slavit's skillfully written chapters gently convey various situations that many children face today. The book covers incidents from kindergarten, to first love, the school bully, all the way up to college acceptance. Larry's actions deeply reflect how important his family is to him.

Teenagers reading this book will be able to relate to, and be guided by, many of the stories.

Larry Chu Jr.'s childhood lessons have served him well.

Paul D. Nyberg
Publisher and owner of the Los Altos Town Crier

Norma's book, *Pork Buns and High-Fives,* is a charming story. It is a "page-turner" that I recommend for both children and adults. There is a strong respect for Larry's parents woven throughout the book, and the reader gets a glimpse of Chinese culture as Larry Chu develops into a fine young gentleman.

The book includes Chef Chu's recipe for pork buns, which I look forward to trying.

Louise Webb
Retired reporter, Saratoga, California
Memoir Instructor – Saratoga, California

Book Dedication by Larry Chu

In appreciation to my parents, Ruth and Lawrence, for their guidance and support.

Their high standards, honesty, and strong work ethics are the lessons that I hope to pass down to my son, Larry III.

Book Dedication by Norma Slavit

To my grandchildren, Ilana, Rachel and Joshua.

To my grandchildren's dear parents, Joel, Betsy, Lisa and Steve.

To the memory of my beloved parents, Rose and Max.

And to the blessed memory of my dear husband, Herb.

Special Acknowledgements

A note of appreciation to my fiancée, Paul Staschower, for his support and love.

Thank you to Luanna Leisure who has been here for me through the publishing process.

Letter from Larry Chu

Dear Readers,

I hope you enjoy the childhood stories Norma has written about in this book, as much as I have enjoyed reliving the experiences through her words. Reading these childhood stories has brought back many memories growing up a Chinese American boy in the Bay Area. Although the names of the characters have been changed in respect for individual privacy, I'm sure many people reading this book will recognize themselves and the memories we shared together.

Growing up in school, I often felt like an outsider trying to fit in a world to which I didn't seem to belong. Looking back at those stories now, I realize the role my experiences played in shaping my personality and helping me become the person I am today.

Many people have told me how similar these stories are to their own childhood. Opening my lunch box to find my favorite homemade snack, only to be mocked and laughed at by classmates, apparently wasn't limited to me, or to Chinese food.

My hope is, someone going through these same issues today will realize how common and natural these feelings are, and that they are not alone.

It took a lot of courage for my parents to leave China and build a new home in the United States. I thank them for sharing their experiences and for the valuable lessons they passed on to me.

My Mother taught me that most intolerance comes from lack of experience and exposure to things that are different. She believed that one of the best ways to overcome prejudice is to reach out to people and try to build connections. In this way, people may begin to understand we are more alike than different.

I hope, that by sharing my story, people will realize how important acceptance and understanding is to creating harmony and peace in the diverse and integrated culture in which we live today.

Larry Chu

Summer, 2019

A Note From Norma Slavit

I choose to write about Larry Chu's memoirs, because his story is an inspiring one for young students. His parents, Ruth and Chef Chu, are founders of Chef Chu's renowned Chinese restaurant located at the epicenter of Silicon Valley in Los Altos, California.

His parents emphasized the importance of being honest, loyal and respectful – traits that helped Larry deal with life. Many of the issues Larry faced are similar to those that trouble young people today: how to deal with disappointments, being different, dealing with the class bully and how to help someone who has been diagnosed with medical problems such as cancer and autism.

This story is a collection of memoirs, examples of coping skills that helped an Asian boy growing up in Silicon Valley. In this book, the reader shares memorable experiences including a trip when Larry's parents were invited to the White House, Larry's unique school political campaign, and experiencing the devastating Hong Kong typhoon.

Working with Larry to share the memoirs for this book has been a rewarding pleasure and delight for me. It is fitting that I choose to write Larry's story now, when Chef Chu's Restaurant celebrates a significant anniversary. The year 2020 marks a milestone of 50 successful years in the greater San Francisco Bay Area, a record few Chinese restaurants can match.

Today, Larry is Chef Chu's general manager and partner. One can find him in the restaurant pausing to chat with some of the myriad of patrons who dine at their renowned restaurant every day. With his warm, charismatic personality and genuine concern for people, Larry continues his Father's tradition – to make every dining experience like "grand opening day," and to treat guests like family.

Chef Chu's has been my preferred Chinese restaurant for the past 25 years. The popular Chinese chicken salad and the Mu-Shu vegetables are two of my favorites. And, by the way, when you go there, ... tell them Norma sent you.

Chapter 1

Differences

Bang!

Down crashed the top of Larry's lunch box, narrowly missing Billy's finger.

"Hey. That's my finger you almost smashed," Billy called out. "You don't have to get mad just because I want to see what you have in your lunch."

"Something in there smells funny. Come on, Larry, show us your lunch," Sam elbowed Larry.

Billy and Sam sat next to Larry in the kindergarten class at Edison School. It was lunch time, and the second week in kindergarten. Boys and girls were hurrying to explore the contents of their lunches. Tinfoil and plastic wrappings flew in the air as the children made a mad rush to get to their food.

"Yuck," giggled Sam holding his nose.

Larry kept his lunch box closed.

"Something is very smelly in Larry's lunch," chanted Sam.

"It smells gross," added Billy.

"Yeah, weird," Sam agreed, pretending Larry wasn't able to hear what they were saying.

"What is in there?" Billy and Sam finally asked Larry when they couldn't control their curiosity any longer.

"Why did you close your lunch box? Aren't you hungry?" continued Billy.

"Don't you know it's lunch time? Come on, I'll let you look at my jelly sandwich if you let me see what's in your lunch," Billy tried once again to get Larry's attention.

This time, the boys got Mrs. Greenly's attention. The kindergarten teacher walked over to check the commotion.

"What's going on boys? Is there a problem I can help you with?"

"Larry's not eating his lunch, Mrs. Greenly," replied Sam.

"Yeah, and there is something very weird in there," added Billy pointing to Larry's lunch box, but keeping his finger a safe distance away.

The teacher turned to Larry, "Is there anything wrong?" she asked him.

"No, Mrs. Greenly. Everything is fine I just don't feel so good today. Not hungry at all," he replied turning away from her.

The teacher bent down, and spoke quietly to Larry, "I understand. That can happen. Sometimes we are not hungry. I know how you feel."

In a few minutes, the teacher returned with a small carton of cold milk and a graham cracker. She placed the food down on top of Larry's lunch box.

"Never can tell," she began. "You might get hungry later." Larry thought he saw Mrs. Greenly wink at him before she walked away.

"Thank you, Mrs. Greenly," he called out to her.

When the school bell rang, announcing a short day, Mrs. Chu was waiting for her son. Larry was in a hurry to get in the car. "Hi, Mom. Let's get going," he greeted her.

"What's the rush? I am anxious to hear how your day went and how you liked your lunch," remarked Mother. "Tell me about school this morning."

"Nothing much happened. Can we go home now?" Larry pleaded.

"I want you to tell me what happened at lunch time, Larry Chu. Did you find the treat I put there?"

Larry assumed he was in trouble now, because Mother called him by his first and last name. But, Mother didn't say a word, she just gave him a stern look that seemed to freeze her face and eyes in an icy glare. "Okay, okay, your pork buns are always delicious, really great – just please don't ever make them again for my lunch."

3

"Why, Larry, did someone say something to you?" Mother's icy stare began to melt away as she spoke.

"Nothing happened. Anyway, I don't want to talk about it," he replied.

"Then we'll talk about it when we get home," she said to Larry. "We'll talk about it when we get home."

They drove the rest of the way in silence. When they got home, Larry hid his lunch box on the counter top behind his mother's cookbooks. She brought out an apple and a cookie and placed it in a dish in front of Larry. He ate in a hurry, but it didn't seem to fill the empty feeling in the pit of his stomach.

"Gee, thanks for the snack, Mom," said Larry. "I think I'll go to my room now and play with my new Lego set."

"Not so fast, son. I want to talk to you about school. Remember?"

"Latter, Mom. Let's talk a little latter," Larry answered on his way to his room.

While Larry was in his room, Mrs. Chu looked around for his lunch box. Finding it behind her cookbooks, she quickly opened the box to get it ready for the next day. To her surprise, she found the uneaten pork buns. She fluffed them up and warmed them in a steamer. The sweet, warm smell filled the kitchen. Mrs. Chu placed them in a dish on the

4

kitchen table, and walked out of the room.

The smell of pork buns traveled from the kitchen across to Larry's room. He opened his door a crack wide enough for him to peak into the room. No one was there. Following the sweet, savory scent to the plate on top of the table, Larry quickly gobbled down two pork buns that were in the dish.

He had just finished eating when Mother walked back into the room. "Sure glad to see you still like my pork buns," she said noticing they were gone.

"Sure, Mom, but I only want to eat them at home."

"There must be a reason why you didn't eat them at lunch time," said Mother. "Let's talk about it, son."

Larry could tell his mother was not going to drop the subject. "Gee, it was nothing, really, Mom. Just wasn't hungry," he replied.

"Larry Chu! Pork buns are your favorite, and I made this one especially big for you. I would like to know what happened." Larry noticed Mother's eyes began to have that icy glare again.

"Okay, okay. There's a kid in my class . . . a . . . a . . . a boy who never ever saw a pork bun in his entire life. He said it smelled weird. Billy said it was *gross.* And, that's what happened today."

"That must have felt hurtful," replied Mother. "If Billy and the other boy knew how good pork buns taste, they probably wouldn't have said those things. Say, that gives me an idea. Why don't we ask them over next week for a play day, and I'll make some pork buns for everyone. Larry, what do you think about my idea?"

"Sure, Mom. Sure. Just don't ever put pork buns in my lunch again."

"I heard you, son. Once that boy tries the new food, he'll realize it's not so different from potato dumplings that his mother probably makes. You can give them our phone number and I'll talk to their mothers tomorrow."

"Wait a minute. Why do you want to talk to their mothers?" Larry asked. "Talk? Talk about what? Not the teasing?"

"No, Larry. I won't talk to them about what happened in class today. Just want to give directions to our house."

"That's different. Okay then." Larry started to get up once more.

"Just one more thing," Mother continued. "Do those boys tease anyone else in class?"

"Sometimes," Larry replied. "Once I heard them tease Sara and Max. But, only a little. Raymond Gotfried wears a little cap on his head. He called it a word I can't pronounce, something that sounds like yam-u-kah. It has something to do with his religion. And Sara wears such thick eye glasses. Once I heard someone call her, 'Sara Four Eyes.' Lucky for them the teacher never heard that one."

"Let's include them also on the play day when we have Sam and Billy here. You can show all of them your new Lego set. I may even let them help me make the pork buns," suggested Mother.

"Sounds, like a great plan, Mom. Thanks." Hoping the conversation was over, Larry walked quickly back to his room. The matter was settled.

From that day to the end of the kindergarten school year, Mother made peanut butter, jelly and once in a while a cheese sandwich – but never again did she put pork buns in Larry's lunch.

Author's Note:

Pork buns are a favorite food among Chinese. Often white in color, they can be large as the palm of one's hand, usually steamed, slightly sweet and fluffy. Pork buns can be filled with savory pork, another meat or a vegetarian mixture. Sometimes they are sold in a Chinese bakery, and are available in most Chinese restaurants.

Chapter 2

Making Sense Instead of Cents

Mrs. Chu held the dollar bill up, waving it high in the air like a small Fourth of July flag. "Look what I found," she said to her six-year-old son, holding the money a little beyond his reach.

Larry jumped as high as he could, trying unsuccessfully to retrieve it. "Thanks, Mom. I was looking all over for that."

"Not so fast. First, I have a question. Where did this money come from?"

"I earned it," answered Larry.

"You **earned** it?" she accentuated Larry's words. "How?"

"Oh, it's a long story," Larry tried to end the conversation.

"We have all afternoon, *Niu-niu*," *(Pronounced nu-nu, an endearing word many Chinese mothers call their children.)* Mrs. Chu pulled over a chair for Larry and motioned for him to sit down next to her. "I'm not going anywhere and you're not going anywhere either. Let's talk about it right now."

It was Friday afternoon and Mrs. Chu was busy with the family laundry. Sorting the family clothes, she was careful to remove paper clips, rubber bands and other buried treasure from her children's clothes. That's when she found something stuffed deep in the back of Larry's shirt pocket. Carefully, she unfolded the paper, and was surprised to find a dollar bill.

Moments before, Mother had called her son into the laundry room.

"You called me, Mom. Is something wrong? Need help with the laundry?" Larry asked. He was always the first one to volunteer when help was needed.

"No, son. I want to know *where* this dollar came from."

Larry answered her question again, quickly, "I earned it, Mom."

"I know you said you *earned* it, but I want to know *how* you earned it. Don't worry if it's a long story, we have all afternoon."

"But, Mom," he began trying to cut the conversation short, "I have my first grade spelling words to study." Mother continued speaking in a firm tone. "Just start from the beginning."

Larry decided to try and stretch out the details since it was almost time for him to practice the piano and he was in no rush to start.

"Well," began Larry. "It all happened in our backyard," he pointed to the fishpond. "A few days ago I fished out some smooth, shiny rocks. I put the best one in my pocket thinking it would make an excellent skipping stone. I'll tell you what a skipping stone is a little later." He continued his story dramatizing it as he went along. "At recess, the next day all the boys in the first grade classes were talking about skipping stones, that's when I pulled out my rock. The sun hit it just right and made that rock shine almost like a smooth piece of colored glass. Bobby Frank asked if he could look at it, so I let him. Well, he turned that rock over and over again in his hands watching it catch rays of the afternoon sunlight."

"Sure would like to have one of these. Where did you get it Larry?" Bobby asked me. "Do you have another one?"

"Nope," I said trying to avoid Bobby's first question. "This is my one and only. Not another one like it."

Bobby was very curious, and he kept talking, "Sure would like to own one like that. Are you willing to sell it to me?"

I took my time answering his questions, and continued, "I never thought of selling it because it would make an excellent skipping stone. It's one-of-a-kind you know," I told him.

"Come on, Larry. Will you or won't you sell it to me?"

"Are you sure you want this particular one-of-a-kind stone

or maybe something a little smaller or less smooth and shiny?" I asked. "That's when he shook his head, *no.*"

"Then I pretended to fish around my pocket like I was looking for another stone."

"Look, Larry, this is the one I want. I'll give you one dollar for it, not a penny more."

"I tried hard to remove the surprised look that must have been on my face. Then with a deep sigh I repeated Bobby's question. One dollar? I left the question dangling in mid-air. At that point, the situation called for some quick thinking. I didn't want to scare off Bobby, and I didn't want to give him time to change his mind, so . . ."

Mother interrupted Larry's story, "Could you get to the end of the story, Larry, my laundry is waiting and it's time for your piano practice."

"Sure, Mom. Well, you see it was this way . . ." The first grader continued. "Seeing that Bobby really wanted that rock, I started to polish it against my t-shirt. Then, I looked Bobby straight in the eye and said, sold to Bobby Frank for one dollar, the only skipping stone of this here kind in the city of Los Altos, State of California."

Mrs. Chu listened to every word her son related before interrupting, "That's not the story I was thinking of when you said you earned the dollar. I thought maybe you were

11

going to tell me you did the dishes or helped mow the neighbor's lawn. You know, Larry, your friend could have found a rock by himself, and **you** didn't have to pay for it so how fair was it to ask Bobby to pay for it?" Mother's voice began to get louder, "Do you understand what I am saying Lawrence Chu, Jr.?"

"Yes, Mom. I think you are suggesting I buy it back from him and return his dollar. But, Bobby is so set on that rock I don't think he would let me buy it back."

Larry saw that steel gaze in his mother's eyes, the same look Chinese mothers sometimes use when they are disciplining their children. The look spoke louder than any words. She continued, "I wasn't suggesting you buy it back. You shouldn't either. Do you know why?"

Larry paused for a moment then answered her question thoughtfully, "Guess it was like, well maybe taking advantage of him, a little."

"Keep going Larry." Mother put her arm gently around his back and drew him closer. "What's the right thing to do in this case?"

"Give him back his money?" The words came out like a question, not an answer. Larry looked up and saw a sudden frown sweep across his mother's face. He continued firmly, "Yes, I'll give him back his dollar." Mother's frown turned into a hard, steel gaze again. Larry tried hard to swallow, then added, "I'll give him back his dollar **tomorrow!**"

"And, what else?" Mrs. Chu was waiting for the answer she wanted to hear.

"But, Mom, that rock was on our property so legally it belongs to me." He tried not to look up, but from the corner of his eyes he could see his mother's expression hadn't changed. He continued in a voice that was barely audible, "I will tell Bobby Frank he can have his money back and that he can **keep t**he rock too."

"What did you say, Larry?"

Larry repeated his reply, this time in a louder voice.

"I thought you would come up with the right answer, *Niu-niu.* You always do!" The steel-hard gaze was gone from his mother's eyes, and Larry felt better.

Mother continued, "Now that we understand each other, I won't keep you a minute more. Let me set the timer to 30 minutes so you can start your piano practice right now."

Larry turned to walk away, paused and added in a matter-of-fact tone, talking to himself, "Guess maybe it wasn't a one-of-a-kind rock after all."

Chapter 3

Gentleman's Agreement in a Candy Shop

Dinosaur eggs! That's what the candy jawbreakers were called. The dinosaur eggs were what Larry and his friends bought most often when they visited their favorite candy store on El Camino Real.

Mr. G's candy store was the most popular store in town, especially the weeks before Valentine's Day. Mr. G always had tempting free samples ready. Larry parked his bike in front of the store and went up to the front door with great anticipation. Slowly, he opened the door allowing a little bell above him to jingle, announcing his presence.

Today, ice cream was the first item of business on Larry's list. With the confidence of a seasoned shopper, he sauntered over to the counter to check out the flavor of the month. Chocolate chip mint. Larry's favorite! It hadn't changed since last week. Licorice was next on the list. The label read, "Red Vines." Checking it out, Larry smiled in approval when he noticed the vines were still ten cents a stick.

Larry noticed that Mr. G received some new dinosaur eggs. They had swirls of bright colors that boasted every hue of the rainbow. The sweet smells of candy and ice cream

14

wafted through the store sticking to everything, even the hot red and pink valentine decorations. Larry was trapped in a sugary state of euphoria. He closed his eyes for a moment and let the sweet smells envelope him. Mr. G broke the spell by pushing a silver tray of chocolate marshmallow samples in front of Larry.

"Give me your opinion of this new candy," Mr. G insisted, bringing the ten-year old boy back into the moment. "And say, if you are looking for something new and different for Valentine's Day, Larry, take a look over here." Mr. G got Larry's attention as he tapped on the glass counter and pointed to the top shelf with his long, bony finger. Larry was busy evaluating the candy sample as he let his tongue brush away any remnants of chocolate from his lips.

"Wow," Larry exclaimed. "Looks like a giant Hershey's Candy Kiss."

"Want to see it?" asked Mr. G. Not waiting for an answer, the candy shop owner climbed up a little step ladder and brought down a giant candy kiss wrapped in shiny, crinkly, silver paper just like the smaller candy kisses. He placed it on the empty counter right in front of Larry.

"Sure," replied Larry after the fact. "Wow, never saw anything like that before."

"It's one-of-a-kind, my only one. People who like something different have been looking at it ever since it came in for Valentine's Day. It's five pounds of pure, chocolate heaven. Sweet enough to turn any young lady into your special valentine. Here, look at it up close."

"Wow, this is a big one," Larry announced. "Biggest one I have ever seen. It must be as big as my backpack. How much?" inquired Larry who by now was turning it around and around admiring it from all angles.

"For you, son, for you . . . it's $10.95 because you're my ice cream and licorice regular customer."

"Sure would like it but I have to go home and check my piggy bank."

"I understand," began Mr. G. "Come back after you've checked your money and let's just hope it's still here. You understand, I can't promise it will be. If someone comes in and has money to buy it . . ." Mr. G stopped short and stared directly into Larry's wide open eyes without blinking. "I hope you understand." With that, he climbed back on the ladder and placed the huge candy kiss in its prominent spot for all to admire. "Now, how about something you can afford. We just got in the jawbreakers you like."

Larry wasn't listening to Mr. G. He just kept staring up at the candy kiss. "I know someone who sure would like that.

16

Would you hold it for me until tomorrow?"

"Though I would like to, can't do that son. But, let's look at something you can afford." With that remark, Mr. G took out a tray of red and black licorice sticks. "Here, try one of these samples." Mr. G held out a little heart-shaped basket of broken licorice pieces.

"No thanks." Larry reached into his pocket and took out something. "Look, Mr. G, I have one dollar I was supposed to use on lunch today. Would you take it for a deposit to hold the candy until tomorrow?"

"Well, say there," Mr. G began rubbing his bald head, "It is my one-and-only, and all my customers have been looking at it." Mr. G held his narrow, pointed chin in both hands and seemed in deep thought. He turned to look directly into the boy's wide-open, hopeful eyes. "I don't think anyone has ever asked me to hold something with a deposit. But . . . but, I suppose I could do that." Mr. G took Larry's money, turning it over in his hand and finally putting it in his cash register. He pulled out a little slip of paper and wrote down Larry's name, the date, the item and the cost of the item. "Until tomorrow, then," he said to Larry as he extended his hand for a firm, gentleman's agreement type of handshake.

All the way home on his bike, Larry thought about how he was going to surprise Emily, the fastest runner in his fifth grade class. She was the girl he had a crush on since kindergarten. Emily was the one he wanted to surprise with the giant candy kiss. Once she had it, maybe **then** Emily would notice him at last!

Larry wondered how he was going to surprise her at school. How was he going to convince his mother to give him the money to buy the candy? By the time he reached home, he had it all figured out.

Chapter 4

Larry's Plan for the One and Only

The first part of Larry's plan would be the most difficult. He didn't have much homework, so he sat down and finished it in a hurry.

"How about a nice glass of milk, Larry, to go with some fresh cookies I baked this morning?" Mother asked.

"No thanks, Mom," replied Larry. "I have something urgent to discuss. So if you don't mind, I'll start my half-hour piano practice right now, and that will give us more time to discuss my *urgent* matter."

Mrs. Chu reached out to feel Larry's forehead. Larry pulled away abruptly letting his mother's hand fall to her side. "Just checking to see if you have a fever. Do you feel okay, Larry?" Mother asked. "I mean, when is the last time you turned down my home-baked cookies?"

"Save mine for after dinner," Larry said politely as he left the room and went into the family room to put in the required half-hour piano practice his parents expected from each of their five children. Larry made sure to play his scales first and then music from his piano solo book. On this day, his focus was on the future discussion with his mother, so his fingers took over as he played from memory. The half-hour practice went by quickly, and Larry returned to the kitchen just in time to join the family for the evening meal. When the dishes were cleared away, Mother took Larry aside.

"Your piano practice sounded pretty good today," Mother remarked. "Now, what was so important you wanted to talk about?"

Larry swallowed hard. "Could we go into the other room? This is very private," he said. Larry could feel a big lump make its way up into his neck. He cleared his throat and began. When Larry was sure they were far enough away so that no one could hear them he spoke. "Well, as you know, Mom, Valentine's Day is almost here, and I want to give someone a very special valentine."

Son, you don't have to buy me a special valentine. I always like the ones you make for me best of all."

"Of course, Mom, I will make you a special one, but I'm talking about a valentine for a girl in my class."

"Her name wouldn't be Emily by any chance, would it?" asked Mother.

Larry's face turned a hot pink tone. The expression on his face gave Mother her answer.

"Thought so," surmised Mother. "So how much is this going to cost me?"

"It's one-of-a-kind, Mom. Just the biggest, best Hershey Candy Kiss I have ever seen."

"How much son? I am waiting."

"The way I see it, Mom," Larry began. "All l want is an advance on my allowance."

"How much?" Mother's voice got louder.

Larry answered as fast as he could get the words out in one breath, "$10.95."

"What kind of chocolate candy kiss costs $10.95?" Mother seemed shocked.

"As I said, Mom, it's the biggest one I have ever seen. It's about the size of my backpack. Let me explain. Please sit down, Mom."

"No thanks son. I want to stand to hear this one. It better be good."

Here's the deal." Larry said, "You don't have to pay me any allowance for two whole months – besides which I promise to do all my usual chores."

The room got very quiet. Silence.

"Smart kid to come up with such a plan," Larry thought.

"Smart kid to come up with such a plan," Mother thought to herself. Mrs. Chu was deep in thought for what seemed to Larry to be a long time before she spoke. Then she looked straight into Larry's eyes, as she tackled the problem. "I can see this valentine means a great deal to you, Larry, so my answer is . . . yes. I will advance your allowance next week, but just this one time, do you understand?"

"Next week? Did you say next week, Mom? That will be too late. You see, Mr. G is holding it for me – but only until tomorrow after school. So if you could please give me the money now, I will bike it over to him after class tomorrow."

"Not so fast, son," Mother began. "First place, ten dollars is a lot of money. I don't want you bringing that much to school. Tell you what . . . I will pick you up after class tomorrow and we will go and see Mr. G together."

"That's swell, Mom. But do you have to come into the store with me?" Larry started to realize this wasn't going to be as easy as he thought. He could feel that lump inching back up in his throat again. He swallowed hard. "Can you at least park the car a few doors down the block?"

"Let's not carry this thing too far, Larry. You don't want me to change my mind. I will park wherever I find a space. Now, get a good night's sleep dear."

Larry reached out to give his mother a bear hug around her waist almost throwing her off balance. "I'll take that cookie now." He stretched out his hand to get the cookie then gobbled it down fast. "Thanks, Mom. You're the greatest. And

I promise to do all my chores. Good night." With that Larry skipped off to bed.

Even though Larry closed his eyes tightly, he couldn't fall asleep. All he could think about was the next part of his plan, how to surprise Emily. Before long, another brilliant idea popped into his head. He would hide the candy kiss in his backpack behind the stage curtain in the auditorium. No one ever went into the auditorium at the end of the day unless there was something to rehearse. It was a perfect place to hide the candy kiss inside his backpack. His plan would have to include getting a pass to use the bathroom, after which he would quickly get his backpack, remove the candy, then transfer it to Emily's bike, and return to class.

What a plan. It was fail-proof! Brilliant! Exhausted from the thoughtful planning, Larry fell into a deep sleep.

Chapter 5

Can a Fail-Proof Plan Fail?

The following day, Mother drove Larry to the candy store as she promised. Everything seemed to be working out as Larry planned. So far, so good. Mrs. Chu parked the car, and Larry went into the candy store alone to purchase the Hershey candy. He didn't even open the door twice to hear the welcoming bell jingle.

When Larry entered the candy shop, Mr. G was already wrapping the huge valentine kiss in see-through cellophane paper. Larry moved to the counter and smiled joyfully as he watched Mr. G tie the gift with a colorful, over-sized pink, polka dot bow. It took both of them to place it carefully inside Larry's backpack. It was a tight fit, so tight that Larry and Mr. G could barely pull the zipper closed.

At school, the next day, Larry's plan was to hide the candy in Emily's bike basket before the end of the day. He got to school early and hid his backpack in the auditorium, on the stage behind the curtains. No one was around. "So far, so good," he said to himself as he went to class feeling good about his fail-proof plan.

It was an overcast day, gloomy and windy, the kind of day when it felt like rain was in the air. The school day seemed to drag on. Larry could hardly wait for the last period to arrive. He finished his math paper quickly and turned his head to look outside. A brisk wind was blowing the trees, and one branch made an annoying scratchy sound as it banged against the classroom windowpane. Larry wasn't sure what bothered him more – the heavy feeling of his heart pounding, the sound of the branch brushing against the window or the loud ticking of the class clock.

He watched and listened to the big clock over the blackboard tick away the minutes. When the time was right, he jumped up, handed his math paper to the teacher and asked for a pass to go to the bathroom.

"It's almost time to go home, so hurry back," the teacher said as she handed Larry the pass.

He rushed out of the room, and ran across the yard to the auditorium. Before he opened the door, Larry checked out the bikes neatly resting in slots outside. Yes, there was Emily's pink bike in the same spot she usually parked it.

Now for the next part of Larry's plan. He was in luck. The auditorium door was unlocked. With one giant leap, he skipped over the second and third steps, leaped onto the stage and pulled the curtain aside. Larry looked for his

25

backpack on stage-right. It wasn't there. He thought for sure that was where he hid it. There wasn't much light backstage, except for the back window which was close to the ceiling and it let just enough light in so that Larry could see his backpack was hidden on stage-left. He hurried over and quickly opened the zipper far enough to check and see if the precious contents were still inside. "So far, so good," he thought to himself. Now he had to get back to class before the last bell rang.

Just as Larry was placing the backpack over his shoulder, he heard a loud bang. Then, a louder bang. Could it be the custodian coming to lock the auditorium door for the weekend? Was he going to be trapped here? How was he going to get out? There were two other doors. Bang. Another loud noise. Was the custodian locking all the doors? Would his mother come by to look for him if he didn't come home? Would she call the police? How would he explain what he was doing in the auditorium? Then he thought about the milk and cookies. How many meals would he miss before he was discovered? Now, besides being aware of his heart pounding, Larry's ears were throbbing. He had to make his next move before the custodian locked all three doors.

Larry moved quickly toward the back door, searching for a sign of someone coming into the auditorium, some unknown person who could ruin his entire brilliant plan. He looked all around, but no one was in sight. It was then he realized the custodian wasn't to blame. The wind had blown the doors shut.

"Whew! A lucky break. So far, so good," he said to himself. He raced to the door, and with one giant leap he was outside.

Next, Larry moved toward Emily's pink bike. Hers was the only one with bright colorful streamers attached to the handle bars. He put down his backpack and pried the zipper open. It stuck to the cellophane wrapping. If he pulled too hard, the wrapping might tear. If that happened, the plan would be ruined, and he would never be able to give the valentine to Emily. Larry pulled and pulled until with one strong jerk, the zipper moved. It was a struggle to the finish, but in the end, he got the candy out in perfect condition, and put it in Emily's bike basket. At that moment, there was no one in sight. Plan achieved. His brilliant plan was going brilliantly. "Whew," he sighed heavily. Suddenly he couldn't remember if he had signed the valentine card. "Valentine card? Where was the card?" he asked himself.

In Larry's rush that morning, he had left the card at home. There was no time to make another one. Larry hurried back to class and got into his seat just as the bell rang and everyone started to line up for dismissal. He looked out of the class window, across the yard in time to see Emily walk up to her bike. Suzie joined her. The two best friends often walked their bikes home together. When Emily saw the giant Hershey kiss, Larry could tell by the look on her face she was surprised. Yes, he surmised, Emily was amazed. Even dazzled. She was delighted. He left the classroom and stayed far enough behind so he wasn't noticed, but close enough to hear Emily's last words before she walked off.

"Wow," Larry heard Emily say. "Wow, I have never seen a Hershey Candy Kiss this big in my entire life." Emily's hand fumbled around her basket looking for a card. "There's no card anywhere," she exclaimed.

"You must know who gave it to you. Come on, you can trust me. Who do you think it was?" asked Suzie impatiently. "Best friends don't keep secrets."

"I really don't know, but it's sure the best valentine present I ever got. Who gave it to me is a mystery, unless **you** hid it there in my basket, Suzie. Or maybe **you** know who put it there. Come on, tell . . ."

Suzie looked puzzled. Shocked. She was speechless.

Larry watched the scene unfold. There was no card. He had forgotten it. How would Emily know who gave her the valentine? Maybe she would think it came from the boy who sat in front of her. This was a turn of events he didn't plan on. So far, **not** so good. What was he going to do next?

Chapter 6
Emily, Emily, Emily

"Yes. Yes. I will tell him, poor kid. He must have been devastated." Mother was on the phone when Larry got home from school. "Thanks for calling. Good-bye."

"Hi, Mom. Just heard the end of your phone conversation. Who is devastated?" he asked. "What happened? Did someone get hurt?" Larry gave Mother a big hug, then collapsed on the kitchen chair, in front of a tall glass of milk and two cookies.

"No one is hurt," she replied trying to change the topic quickly. "Today was a special day for you. How did things go?"

"Oh, a . . . I was first to finish the math quiz."

"You know that's not what I mean, Larry. Did you give Emily the valentine?"

"Yes and no," replied Larry.

"What do you mean yes and no? What kind of answer is that?"

"Well, yes, I put the candy in her basket, but no, I forgot the card. Now, she will never know who gave her that huge ten dollar Hershey Kiss."

"She knows, dear," said Mother in a matter-of-fact tone.

A puzzled expression swept across Larry's face. "Who could have told her?"

"Emily's mother told her," answered Mrs. Chu. "Mothers have a way of knowing things, besides she and I were talking when you walked in the door. Now, have some milk and tell me about your day."

Larry told his mother how he was almost trapped in the auditorium. He dramatized the story a little, emphasizing his problem and disappointment. "Sorry, but I don't want to talk about it anymore. Got to do my homework."

Larry was glad when dinner time came. Sitting down to the family dinner was usually the highlight of Larry's day. Often that was when his grandmother came over to spend time with the family. On this night, Larry barely touched his noodles, except to snake them around in his plate.

"Chi-fan, Chi-fan," Grandmother called out in Chinese, telling Larry to eat.

"Not hungry tonight," he answered her in an endearingly tone of voice.

Larry wasn't in the mood for anything tonight – not even playing with his favorite Lego set. But, something was about to happen that would change his dreary mood. It was a phone call. No one answered the phone, until the third ring.

That's when Mother called out to Larry. "Phone call for you, son," she announced. "Take it in the hallway."

"Hello, this is Larry speaking. Who is it?"

No one replied for a minute or two, then a faint voice responded, "Hello, Larry, this is Emily. How are you?"

"Fine, I guess," he replied.

Then, there was silence. Larry could hear Emily breathing, so he knew she was still on the line. "Larry, my mother told me to call you. She told me **you** were the one who gave me that big Hershey valentine. Thank you. "

"You're welcome," was the only thing Larry could think of to say.

"Goodbye," said Emily. That was the whole conversation. Then, Emily was gone.

Larry had a big smile on his face when he hung up. He felt all the effort – foregoing his allowance, getting the candy, feeling trapped in the auditorium, and hiding the valentine in her bike basket had all been worth it. Now, she finally knew he existed, and he had a real phone conversation with her. The big smile was still on Larry's face when he went into the kitchen where his mother was putting away the dinner dishes.

"Short phone call?" his mother asked.

"Yep, now Emily knows I am the one who gave her the candy. And, she sure seems to like it. At last, she knows I exist."

"Glad you are in a better mood. It's been a long day for you. Why don't you go to bed early tonight dear? I'll be in a little later and we can review your book report, if you would like. Good-night son."

It had been quite a day for Larry, a series of events he would long remember for many years. At the end of the day, everything seemed to have turned out all right. As some of his friends would say, "So far, so good."

So far, so good, Larry thought until he noticed his mother acted a little strange the following week. Almost every day she had a treat ready for him when he came home from school. One day there was a fancy napkin covering his plate. When he removed the lace napkin, usually reserved for company, he found a steaming hot pork bun.

"Chinese New Year is months away, so what's the special occasion, Mom?" Larry asked pulling out a huge, puffy pork bun from the steaming bamboo basket. "Wow, what a great treat. My favorite. Wait a minute. What's going on?" he asked.

"Nothing's going on, you've just been doing so well at school, I thought you might enjoy a special treat," Mother explained. "Go ahead eat, *Chi-fan.*"

Larry took a few bites, then downed some cold milk. He chewed the pork bun slowly, savoring each bite. Then he pried a few large pieces of the soft, warm dough out with his fingers and placed them in the palm of his hand. He smiled at his creativity as, one by one, he popped the pieces of soft dough into his mouth.

"Hmm, by the way, Larry there is something I want to discuss with you."

"Oh, oh . . . here it comes," thought Larry.

"Your teacher talked to Mrs. Anderson and they would like some boys and girls from your fifth grade class to volunteer to take dance lessons in the evening."

"Not interested, Mom," the answer came faster than Larry could swallow the rest of the treat.

"It will be fun, and good exercise too," said Mother in a convincing tone.

"Then, let some of the other kids have the fun and exercise. I'm not interested. Tell you what I am interested in though – these pork buns are the best. Another one please."

Mother held another bun just beyond Larry's reach. She continued, "Emily and Susie will be very disappointed if you are not there."

"How do you know they will be there?" Larry asked getting more interested.

"Mothers talk on the phone. We compare notes."

"I don't care who will be there," Larry continued while eating. "Emily? Did you say Emily? Do you know that Emily will be there for sure?"

"As I was saying, her parents also volunteered to be greeters. Your father and I will drop you off, and Kareem's mother will drive you home. Did I mention that your best friend Kareem is going also and they have a dance party at the end?"

Before Larry could ask another question, Mother continued, "Good. It's settled. This weekend we can look for some appropriate new clothes."

"Clothes?" Larry asked. "I don't need new clothes. Besides, you know I don't like to go shopping." Larry was ready to back out of the whole plan.

"We'll leave early Larry, so you will have the rest of the day free. Wearing a dark blazer, new shirt and a tie, you will look great. Emily will think so too." Mother stopped and waited for that special look of approval to appear on Larry's face. When she saw he was still frowning, she added, "Shopping may take up so much time Larry, that . . . tell you what . . . let's skip your piano practice for this one time. Is that okay, dear?"

He wondered if he heard his mother correctly. Did she say skip piano practice? Before she changed her mind, he replied, "I suppose so, Mom, as long as we only shop in one store."

"Don't push your luck, dear. Good night Larry."

Larry sauntered off to his bedroom thinking that if Kareem and Emily would be there, maybe things wouldn't be so bad after all. It was another chance to see Emily. In the middle of the night, Larry woke up from a scary dream. In it, Emily choose Kareem for a dance partner and Mrs. Anderson picked him.

Author's Note: The word, *Chi-fan*, used here, is a Chinese word politely urging someone to eat.

Chapter 7

Night of the Big Dance

Larry complained about going to Mrs. Anderson's dance lessons, and counted the days when they would be over; but it was fun to spend time with Kareem and Emily. His mother told Larry that while the boys and girls thought they were only learning dance lessons, they were also practicing important character traits such as proper etiquette, good manners, politeness, dignity and modesty.

Larry was glad when time came for the culmination dance party, and he looked forward to the night of the big dance on the hill. It was a chance for Emily to see him in his new blazer and slacks. He was ready an hour before the event. Checking things out, Larry looked in the mirror from all angles and was smoothing down his slick, dark hair when Mother walked into the room.

"Very nice," she exclaimed. "Very nice indeed. I have a handsome son. Are you ready to leave?"

Larry's face turned a shade of red. "Not bad at all," he said to himself, taking one last look in the mirror. "Ready!"

On the drive up to the house on the hill, Larry looked in the car mirror one more time, pressed his new blazer with his hands, straightened his tie and combed his dark hair again. He was deep in thought and smiled at his reflection in the mirror.

Mother interrupted his thoughts, "Remember what I said now, Larry. When you greet each parent, look at them directly in the eye, and always give them a firm hand-shake. It shows good character."

"I don't want to hurt anyone's hand, Mom."

"You will not hurt anyone. Remember, a firm handshake. It shows confidence."

Larry had no way of knowing then, but decades later, he would shake the hands of presidents, city officials, movie stars, and other celebrities who would someday dine at his father's renown restaurant.

As Mother drove up the long driveway, Larry noticed all the lights were glowing from Mrs. Anderson's house. He thought the house looked different at night. He felt different too, a little older and a little taller. He could hear music playing when Mother dropped him off in front of Mrs. Anderson's house. "Have a good time, son," Mother called out as Larry left the car. "Remember, a firm handshake. Bye."

The music playing made Larry think it was an "old person's party," not one for kids. But the next moment, he changed his mind. All the boys and girls were dressed in Sunday-best clothes. He sighed, took a deep breath, threw his shoulders back and entered the house on top of the hill.

Just as Mrs. Anderson had told them, there was a line of parents waiting to greet them. Looking at the name tag the first parent was wearing, Larry smiled, looked the woman squarely in the eye and said, "Pleased to meet you, Mrs. Wilson. My name is Larry." He extended his hand and gave Mrs. Wilson a firm handshake.

Mrs. Wilson was impressed. She turned to her husband and whispered, "Fine young man."

"I did something right," thought Larry. He was off to a good start. So far, so good.

When all the students had arrived, the parents sat down around the side of the room and six boys lined up across from six girls. The girls wore white gloves and pastel colored frilly dresses. Lacey socks neatly covered the top of the girls' black patent shoes. The boys shifted places for a moment, trying to line up across from the girl they wanted to be their partner.

As soon as the first dance was announced, Larry approached Emily, smiled and asked in his grown-up voice, "May I have this dance, Emily?"

"Certainly," she replied smiling shyly.

The next thing Larry remembered is that they were dancing. There was a lovely, sweet, flower-like smell about her. Larry thought Emily must have been wearing perfume. For the moment, he didn't know what to say.

Emily, on the other hand, did know what to say, "You sure look nice in that jacket, Larry."

"Thanks, so do you. I mean . . . that's a lovely dress you are wearing, Emily."

"Thanks," she replied.

Then Larry thought he heard a very soft voice say, "Ouch." He wondered if he had stepped on Emily's foot.

"Are you okay, Em?" asked Larry worried about her foot.

"Oh, it's nothing," she replied. "I am fine." She wasn't sure if her shoes were fine, but she smiled anyway.

The two continued the dance in silence. When the waltz ended, Larry took Emily by the arm. "Let's check out the foaming bubbly drink. May I get you a glass of punch?"

"I would like that," answered Emily.

A line had already formed at the punch bowl where a block of strawberry ice cream was floating in the middle of the punch. The frosty bubbles made Larry thirsty. Mrs. Whitehead stood over the punch filling fancy cups for the students. Larry gave the first drink to Emily and waited for Mrs. Whitehead to fill another cup. Just as Emily and Larry turned to get out of the long line that had formed behind them, Billy Whitehead accidentally bumped into Emily's punch sending it sailing through the air and landing on Larry's new slacks.

"Oops," sighed Billy.

"Oh, dear," exclaimed Emily. "I am so sorry, Larry." Quickly, Emily took out her fancy handkerchief and tried to wipe the punch from Larry's stained blazer.

"It's okay, Em. Accidents do happen," he exclaimed. "No problem." He backed away, and pretended not to notice the red spots that were also on his new slacks.

The two were finishing the last dance when some parents started arriving to pick up their children. "Thanks for the dance," Larry said to Emily, escorting her back to her chair. "Kareem's mother is here to take me home. See you in class Monday."

Mrs. Abdul took one look at Larry's slacks and sighed, "Oh dear, I hope your slacks are washable."

Larry was quiet all the way home, except to thank Mrs. Abdul for the ride.

Mother was waiting for Larry when he returned. "Hope you had a nice time dear," she began, "How was it?"

"It was okay. The punch drink was really good," he replied.

41

"Yes, I see that by looking at your slacks," she said shaking her head.

"It was an accident. I accidentally bumped into someone. But don't worry, Mom. If they have to go to the cleaners, take the money out of my allowance."

"Larry, you always come up with the right thing to say." Mother continued, "Howard stayed up to see you."

"Yeah," said Larry's younger brother Howard. "You look beautiful."

"Saved something from the party to give you, Howie," Larry put his hand into his blazer jacket and brought out a chocolate cookie he had saved wrapped in a fancy paper napkin.

"Thanks Larry," Howie said as he took the cookie and began to eat it. "You look beautiful," he remarked, giving his older brother a big hug good-night. "Beautiful," Howie repeated as he left Larry's room.

Chapter 8

"A" is for Autism

"Chi-fan. Chi-fan."

Larry used a Chinese word he knew Howard understood. He said, *"Chi-fan"* when he wanted someone to hurry and eat. *"Chi-fan,"* he urged his nine-year old brother, Howard, to finish breakfast. "Howard, come on. Eat or you will be late for school. I'll be late too."

"Don't want to go," came Howard's reply.

Of all the brothers and sisters, Larry was the most patient with Howard. Maybe it was because he was three years older, or maybe it was because of Larry's compassionate personality.

"Why don't you want to go?" asked Larry. The bus for special education students stopped in front of their door. It picked up children with special needs like those with autism. The school bus was scheduled to arrive in 15 minutes.

"Howard, you know the bus driver and everyone at school likes you. They will miss you if you don't get on the bus."

"Don't want to go."

"But, why, Howard? Is the teacher mean?" Larry asked as he moved the cereal bowl closer to his brother.

"No."

Is the bus driver mean to you?

"No."

"Then why don't you want to go to school this morning?"

Howard looked up into Larry's smiling eyes, "Gordon always screaming."

"Screaming?" Larry questioned.

"Yeah," Howard replied in his usual matter-of-fact tone.

"Howard, you have to be patient with Gordon," Larry continued trying to assure his brother. "And, Chris says same thing over and over and over. Don't like that."

Trying hard to convince his brother, Larry brought up another subject. "Howie, Friday is pizza day, remember?"

"Yeah."

When Larry didn't get the positive response he was waiting for, he quickly changed the subject again. "Guess what Howie? I have a special treat for you in my lunch." Larry opened his lunch pail to reveal the treat.

"Not going on the bus. Not going to school." Howard said convincingly.

Larry looked up at the kitchen clock, then down at Howard. Carefully, Larry took the treat out of his lunch pail and inched it close to his brother. "Look, Howie, it's the kind of fruit roll you like so much." Larry moved the treat closer. At

last he got a smile from Howard.

"Maybe I'll go this **one time**," said Howard joyfully taking the treat. "Thanks, Larry."

Not wasting a moment, Larry got behind Howard's chair to help him out.

"Let's get going. I'll walk you to the . . . ."

Howard hesitated, then added, "Mary has tantrums."

"Well," Larry began, "sometimes we have to be patient, Howard. Mary can't help it. It's not her fault. Remember how patient Mom was with me when I accidentally knocked over the orange juice on her favorite tablecloth?"

"Yeah," Howard remembered. "Not your fault, Larry. Mom is patient. What else is in your lunch, Larry?"

Worried that Howard might change his mind at any moment, Larry moved to the high pantry shelf where he knew a few hidden treats were stashed. Playing Howard's favorite hide-and-seek game, Larry sang out, "I know where there's a Kit-Kat candy bar. Hide your eyes, Howard. Don't peak."

Howard held his hands up to cover his eyes, leaving a little peaking space between his second and third finger.

"Oh, look what I found, your favorite." Making the roaring sound of an airplane diving down, Larry allowed the candy to fly on the pretend wings in the back of his hand. "Look,

Howie, the plane is making a perfect landing, right on top of your lunch."

At last, Howard was smiling that adorable-little-boy grin that Larry was waiting for. He gave Howard a chance to put the candy up to his nose to inspect it.

"What do you say, sport? Let's be patient and give school another chance."

"Okay," said Howard, "Just **one more chance**," he replied putting the treasured candy tenderly into his lunch pail.

"Right. Thanks Howie, for being so patient with me."

"Patient," Howard repeated the word.

At last, a breakthrough, thought Larry as he helped his brother from the kitchen chair, and lovingly put his arm around his brother's shoulder. The two boys moved out the front door and down the steps toward the bus stop.

In less than five minutes, the bus was there. The door opened wide and the bus driver warmly greeted Howard, "Happy to see you, Howard," he called out.

When Howard saw the bus driver's extended hand ready to give him a high-five handshake, he jumped on the bus. He greeted the bus driver with a question, "Guess what I have in **my** lunch?" Not waiting for an answer, Howard took one last look back at his brother.

"Bye, Larry," Howard shouted.

"Remember. Be, patient," Larry called back.

"Patient," Howard echoed.

The bus door closed behind him.

Author's Note: Autism is a problem that some "special" needs" children have with verbal and non-verbal communication. They may repeat things often, and show repetitive behavior. To learn more about autism, you might ask a parent, teacher, librarian or your doctor to help you look up the condition in a book.

Chapter 9

It Could Only Happen in America

"Tell us about the Secret Service men, Dad," said Chrissy.

"Yes, Father, and I want to hear the story about meeting the President," requested Jonathan.

"No, Father, start with the invitation to the White House," Jennifer implored.

"Why not start at the beginning, Dad," Larry added his suggestion.

It was the family story time when everyone gathered around the table to listen to Mother and Father talk about their wonderful memories of Chef Chu's Restaurant and the past.

"Yes, yes, I want you to get the facts straight, so I will begin with the phone call," started Father.

"Larry was about 14 at the time, and Ronald Reagan was President of the United States," added Mother.

"Right, right. Say, Luta (Father often used the Chinese Lutu, pronounced "Luta" word for Ruth), who is telling this story anyway?"

"Well, on with it then," answered Mother.

"I remember that phone call well, and the year. It was 1967."

"Was it a phone call for reservations?" asked Jonathan.

"That's what I thought at first, but no." Father acted out the scene pretending to speak into an imaginary phone, "Chef Chu's Restaurant. How can I help you?" Father explained someone on the other end of the phone announced he was Mr. Schultz's assistant and it was important that he speak **directly to Chef Chu**. "Chef Chu here," Father went on.

"The voice on the other end continued, 'Good afternoon, Chef Chu, I am calling for the Honorable Secretary of State, Mr. George Schultz. He is inviting you and your wife to a special State Department event in Washington, D.C. in two weeks.' Then the voice paused for my reply."

"Were you surprised the call was from Mr. Schultz?" asked Jonathan.

"Yes and no," continued Father. "Before Mr. Schultz became the Honorable Secretary of State, he and his family dined frequently in our restaurant. They often celebrated the December holidays in our private dining room. I remember Peking duck was one of his favorite dishes."

"The children aren't interested in the duck, Lawrence dear. On with the story please. It's getting late," Mother reminded him.

"Of course I was surprised and honored he would be calling me all the way from the White House," Father continued the story. "When I got home that night your mother and I discussed the once-in-a-lifetime invitation, of special importance, that we were honored to accept. Who could ever imagine that your parents would be invited to the White House? It could only happen in America," added Father.

"Right," repeated Mother. "Imagine, children, when your dad was a little older than Larry, he left China for America, and six years later, in 1970, he opened a small restaurant here, in Los Altos. We had only a few tables then. Today, fifty years later, we can serve about 800 customers a day. But, back to the story, Lawrence."

"As I recall," said Father, "We had only a short time to get ready. We called Aunt Lois and asked her to come along to be with you, children. We had to get a dress for Mom, I already had a tuxedo, we had to make arrangements for a hotel . . . boom, boom, boom . . . details, details so many details and so little time to prepare," Father tried getting all the words out in one long breath. Excitement flashed in his eyes as if everything had happened only yesterday. "The very next day I returned the phone call to Mr. Schultz's assistant and accepted the invitation. And, before we knew it, we were off to Washington."

"Shorten the story Lawrence, it's getting late and tomorrow is a school day," reminded Mother.

"Yes, yes, yes." Father continued, "After you kids were settled in our hotel room, Aunt Lois took you out to explore Washington while Mom and I got dressed for the lavish state luncheon honoring the Prime Minister of the French Republic and Mrs. Chirac. Mother looked gorgeous and I didn't look half-bad, myself . . ."

"Bragging, Lawrence?" Mother joked.

Father's answer came swiftly, "Well, look at the pictures and judge for yourself," Father said holding up one as he arranged other photos on the kitchen table for all to see.

He continued, "We rushed out to get a taxi and were met by photographers and secret service staff. Once in the State Building, we had to pass through security and then were formally escorted into an elevator that took us to the Benjamin Franklin Ballroom for the special State luncheon honoring the Prime Minister of France."

"Tell us about the fancy ballroom, did you recognize any important people, was Nancy Reagan there?" Chrissy rattled off her questions.

Mother shared her memories, "Not so fast, Chrissy, one question at a time. Before entering the lovely ballroom, your father and I and all the other guests had to pass through the receiving line. Your father proudly walked in . . . just ahead of me. When we got up close to the ballroom door . . ."

"Don't stop there," Larry urged. "Keep going, Mom."

"Well, children," Mother continued sharing her memories. "Just as we approached the entrance, Secretary of State, George Schultz introduced us to the Prime Minister, and I think I heard him say something like, 'Prime Minister Chirac, this is Chef Chu, the **best Chinese Chef in America.**'"

"Wow," said Larry repeating the phrase, "The best Chinese Chef in America?"

Mother continued, "I don't think I will ever forget the magnificent ballroom, the lavish luncheon and so many honored guests that were present. It was a day I will always remember."

"Then, when we got back to our hotel, another invitation arrived," Father continued the story gesturing with his hands.

"Another party for the same day?" Jennifer asked.

"Yes. Yes." remembered Father. "The concierge in our hotel sent someone to our room to deliver an envelope. This one came directly from **The White House**. It was another honor to attend an evening of entertainment scheduled for that night."

"Wow, another party the same day?" asked Howard. "Weren't you tired?"

"Not tired as much as we were excited, son," recalled Mother. "This time we were invited to **The White House**."

Father put more copies of pictures on the kitchen table. One had the official White House seal and read, *The President and Mrs. Reagan request the pleasure of Mr. and Mrs. Chu on Tuesday evening March 31, 1987 at 9:45 o'clock.* Mother got out the entertainment program she had saved over the years. It showed the medley of songs famous singer DIONNE WARWICK sang that evening. The songs included *Do You know the Way to San Jose? Alfie*, and *That's What Friends Are For*. She also included a picture showing Mother and Father dancing.

"Just imagine children, I came to America when I was a little older than Larry; today, I can talk about being at the White House," recalled Father.

"Your father and I danced to Dionne Warwick singing that great song, *What's It All About, Alfie*. We were pretty good dancers too," added Mother.

"You're right, Luta," agreed Father as he winked at her.

"Lawrence, I still have that recording somewhere. Let me get it and play it for the family." Mother left the room for a moment and quickly returned with the record. "Listen, children, this is Dionne Warwick's singing those great songs," said Mother as she turned on the music and began to hum to the words softly.

Larry noticed his brother, Howie, had already fallen asleep.

"Just think about it," Father began to end his story. "Someday one of you will be working in the restaurant at my side as manager of Chef Chu's Restaurant."

Larry could feel his father looking right at him as he spoke. Music in the background was playing, *"What's it all about Alfie,"* and at that moment, being manager and working with his father, was the last thing in Larry's thoughts. High school was in Larry's future, and his thoughts were filled with questions like: How would he fit in? Where would he fit in? As Mother began to sing the lyrics to the song, in his thoughts, Larry changed the words from *"What's it all about Alfie,"* to *"What's it all about, Larry?"*

He would soon find out.

Benjamin Franklin Room

Hon. George Shultz
2008

Picture Bottom of Page 56

Chef Chu, Charlotte Mailliard Shultz, Honorable George Shultz, and Larry Chu. Photo taken in 2008 at Chef Chu's Restaurant in Los Altos, California.

Three Photos Top of Page 57
Left to Right: The President and Mrs. Reagan, Chef Chu, and Chef Chu with Patrick Wayne, the son of John Wayne.

Invitations sent from the White House to Mr. and Mrs. Chu, one honoring the Prime Minister of the French Republic and Mrs. Chirac, March 31, 1987.

Chapter 10

Only at Edison High

The screams, as piercing as they were loud, reverberated down the school hallway. Continuing to scream, the girls dashed away from the frightening scene. A ten-foot long snake slithered out from behind the top of Larry's open locker and crawled down the corridor following them. Larry thought he could still hear the girls' screams as he woke from his nightmare of a dream.

After that, he had a difficult time getting back to sleep. After all, it was Larry's first day at Edison High, and for the past few days his friends had been talking about horror stories they had either heard or made up. He put that out of his mind as he dressed in his favorite orange rugby shirt, ate a quick breakfast, hugged his mother and biked to school.

It was a lovely, sunny, autumn day in Los Altos, California. Leaves from the tall trees that skirted the school driveway were just beginning to fall. Larry enjoyed the gentle morning breeze as he parked his bike on the bike rack, threw his backpack over his shoulder and entered the building.

Many of the students who attended this private school, had been together from grades one through eight. During the short ride, questions raced through his thoughts. Would he see any old friends? Would it be easy to make new friends? What adjustments would he have to make as a freshman?

Walking down the school corridor, he looked around for a familiar face. He turned his head from side to side, and was halfway down the corridor hall when he bumped into something or someone. Looking up, he saw the frowning face of a boy who appeared to him to be six feet tall – six feet of pure muscle.

"Soooory," exclaimed Larry sheepishly tripping over his own feet. The other boy frowned, looked down at Larry, shook his head and said, "Watch where you're goin'."

Moving closer to the wall, Larry concentrated on looking for his first period, homeroom class. He told himself it was late, and better to look for his first period homeroom class than to bother with his locker. There was time for that tomorrow.

After three uneventful periods, the noon lunch bell rang. Once he was out in the school yard, Larry looked around for a friend with whom he could eat lunch. When he couldn't find a familiar face, he sat by himself on a bench. It was then, he began an unscientific study of faces and groups. One group of basketball players caught his attention. They were proudly sporting their colorful team jackets. Larry loved basketball. Thoughts raced in his head. He wondered if he would fit in with them.

Then another group got his attention. These were kids wearing black t-shirts and ripped jeans. "No, that's not a group for me," he concluded. Continuing his unscientific study, his eyes scanned several little groups whom he labeled as the bookworms, the jocks, the cheerleaders, the future prom queen and king and those few who seemed as bewildered as he.

Overcome with the first day excitement, he biked home with a backpack filled with heavy books. After devouring his favorite dinner that Mother had made in honor of the Chu's five children and their first day back at school, Larry lingered behind after his brothers and sisters had left the dinner table. His father, Chef Chu, was busy at the restaurant, so Larry had some time alone with his mother.

"You didn't say much at dinner, Larry. How was the first day?" she asked.

"The usual, I guess. Uneventful, except I don't know where I fit in," Larry answered.

"Fit in? What makes you think you have to *fit in*?"

"Well, there are the jocks, the bookworms, the popular kids and those who don't seem to fit in with any group. I don't know which group will accept me."

"What do you mean, *accept you*? Listen Larry," Mother instructed, "School is not about *fitting in,* just be yourself. You're a great kid. Maybe you will even start a new group. Who knows? When you are friendly to everyone, chances are they will be friendly as well." With that, Mother encouraged Larry to get to bed early so he could face the next day fresh and a little more confident.

Larry took all eight books out of his backpack and let them fall on his bed. Before an hour had passed, he was still looking at one of them when sleep overcame him.

The next day Larry felt much better about school. His mother's words made sense to him. It was day two at Edison High and today Larry Chu was on a mission. His mother had said, "When you are friendly to them, they will probably respond by being friendly to you." He arrived at school 30 minutes early because he had a brilliant idea. "I'll start a campaign and give everyone I see the *high-five hand greeting,*" he told himself.

He put his plan into action. As he walked down the school corridor looking for his locker, he gave a high-five greeting to everyone he saw. He soon found that boys and girls were friendly and smiled back at him when they saw his hand go up to give them a high-five.

As he walked down the long corridor, he paused to look in a glass showcase that featured a group of girls huddled around one short, Japanese girl who was holding a glistening trophy that read, "EDISON GIRLS WINNING SOCCER TEAM." A warm, tingling feeling traveled through his body. He recognized it as a sense of pride he felt for these girls. Another feeling took hold also. He was basking in the success of his high-five campaign, deep in thought, when he found his locker.

After several attempts with the combination, he realized something was wrong. His locker wouldn't open. For a brief moment, he remembered his nightmare, then quickly dismissed it from his thoughts. He gave the metal locker a little bang. Again, it wouldn't open. Then, with clenched fist, he gave the locker several sledgehammer bangs.

"Having locker problems?" asked a friendly voice coming from behind him.

Chapter 11

The High-Five Campaign

Larry turned around quickly to see a girl peering over his shoulder. She was a short, Japanese girl who looked like the girl holding the trophy he had seen in the showcase.

"Most of us have trouble with our lockers after summer vacation," she began. "I'm a senior and once in a while I have trouble too. If you don't mind telling me your lock combination, I'd like to help." The girl had large, bright eyes, the color of his mother's favorite amber necklace. She wore a button down cardigan with the Edison school colors on an embroidered "Block E".

"Thanks," beamed Larry. Then he whispered, "L 22, R 5, L 12." Looking down the hall to see if anyone was within listening distance. He repeated the combination slowly. The lock opened up right away. "Wow," said Larry. "You've got the magic touch. By the way, my name is Larry. Larry Chu."

"My name is Akemi. Akemi Watanabe. You can call me Kimi. I'm the school student body president and I want to welcome you to Edison High. You are a freshman, aren't you?"

Larry's face felt flushed and he couldn't stop a broad grin that began to travel from one ear to the other. "I am. Does it show that much?"

Kimi giggled, "Not at all. I was just guessing."

The winning soccer player who was also the student body president had stopped to help him. Larry was overwhelmed by her friendliness. He decided she was the perfect person to talk to about his new unscientific project. "Do you have a minute before class? I'd like to tell you about a campaign I'm starting."

Kimi nodded her head, "A campaign? Sure."

Larry proceeded to tell Kimi how well his high-five greeting was working.

"Say, Larry, I like your idea. We need people like you on the Student Council," she added. "Larry Chu, I think you should run for some office of the incoming freshman class. As a matter of fact, I have an application in my backpack. Just give me a minute." Before Larry had a chance to think about Kimi's suggestion, she had the application out and into his hands, along with her own flyer.

"You need to fill this out, make a few posters, create a slogan and print some flyers that tell people who you are and which office you are running for. Here's my phone number. Call if there is anything I can do to help. The election is next Friday, so you don't have much time. Better get to it fast. Good luck, Larry Chu."

"Thanks, Akemi Watanabe."

They gave one another the "high-five greeting," turned and walked to their individual classes.

All the way down the school corridor to class, Larry started experimenting with slogans – "Larry Chu – the right one for you. Vote for Larry Chu, the only one for you."

"Larry Chu, Freshman Class President. A vote for Larry Chu – is the only vote for you."

Before walking into class, he took out Kimi's flyer and read it over and over again. It gave him an idea, and a new slogan took over his thoughts as he stood outside his classroom door:

"VOTE FOR LARRY CHU

THE ONLY ONE FOR YOU

LARRY FOR FRESHMAN CLASS PRESIDENT"

The loud, high-pitched bell rang just as Larry opened the classroom door.

"You're late," a voice from somewhere in back of the room shouted out.

The first week of school went faster than Larry could have imagined. He was busy with homework, trying out for the freshman basketball team and working on slogans for his poster, but he took time to share his first week with his mother.

"Can you imagine, Mom? The **student body president** offered to help me with my campaign. Her name is Akemi. She is captain of the winning school soccer team, and she is no taller than I am. She is Asian like us, and she liked my high-five campaign. She said I have to write a speech and give it in front of the assembly in three days. I don't even know which office I should try for," with that Larry paused to take in a deep breath.

"Son, As long as you are putting out all this effort, I say shoot for the top." Her voice was firm and her remarks were like an arrow pointed at its target, straight to the point.

"You mean I should run for president? **Freshman Class President**?"

"Why not? Go for the top spot, son. When you put your mind to it, you can do anything."

Chapter 12

The Class Bully Attacks

Later that evening, Larry's mother helped him design three huge posters that he decorated with the school colors. Carefully, he brought them to school the next morning when he met, Ray, who was waiting for him at his locker. Larry had renewed his friendship with Ray Gotfried, a friend he remembered from kindergarten who once wore a Yamukah. Ray helped him pin the posters up along the corridor walls where students would notice them – one right over the water fountain.

At lunch that day, Ray came running over to him calling out, "Larry, finish your lunch fast, you have to come with me. We've got big trouble."

"Slow down," said Larry. "Catch your breath, then how about explaining what you mean by, trouble."

Larry swallowed his lunch fast, barely taking time to chew his sandwich. Then, the two boys raced back to the corridor where the posters decorated the hallway. Larry gasped in shock when he saw the problem.

Ray pointed to the wall over the water fountain. "That's what I mean by trouble!"

"There's a trouble-maker somewhere who doesn't want you to be class president. He or she diverted water from the water fountain and aimed it at your poster. The water made the paint run and . . . just look at it . . . the poster is ruined."

"Who would have done such a mean thing?" Larry asked.

"Listen Larry, we don't have time to speculate, we've got to take action fast," said Ray as he took the poster down.

"We don't have time to do another poster. What can we do?" asked Larry.

Ray continued to outline his plan. "Call your mother and ask if you can come over to my house. The Head Master will let you make the call, once you explain."

"Then what?" asked Larry searching for an answer.

"Here's my plan, Larry. My mother is a graphic artist. She works from our home two days a week. You're in luck, because today she is home. My mom has paints and everything we need to make a new poster. Under these circumstances she might even help us."

"You're a pal, Ray, a real friend. But, by the time we bike over to your house, make a new poster, and bike back to school, the campus will be locked up," lamented Larry. "Unless . . . unless . . ."

Ray quickly finished Larry's sentence. "Unless . . . *oy vey* . . . unless I call my mother and she can drive over to pick us up."

68

"What's *oy vey?*" Larry asked.

"Oh, it's a Jewish word for a situation like this," answered Ray.

Before Larry could give him a high-five, Ray was on his way down to the Head Master's office.

The two boys took turns explaining the disastrous situation. Before they could get another word in, Mr. Gillespie spoke in a firm voice. "Boys, you were right coming to my office. I want you to know Edison School does not now, and will not ever, tolerate this kind of behavior. We have zero tolerance for bullies. It happens the French Club meets today, so the school will be open for another two hours. I invite you to put up your poster, right here, next to my office door." Mr. Gillespie handed Larry another blank poster and continued, "Please use this phone and call your mothers for permission. You certainly have mine." With that, Mr. Gillespie handed the school phone to Ray.

Understanding the gravity of the situation, Mrs. Gotfried pulled up in front of the office in 10 minutes. Everything was ready for them when they walked into Mrs. Gotfried's home office. Bright colored, thick felt pens were out and there was a large, flat working space on a table.

"I was afraid if you used paints they would not dry in time," remarked Mrs. Gottfried. "Here, use these felt pens instead."

The boys got to work right away. Ray drew a huge fortune cookie, and Larry printed the words: "A bright future for you, when you vote for Larry Chu." The fortune was drawn coming out of the cookie and spread across the middle of the poster. The finishing touches were added and the poster was finished in one hour.

The boys stood back and admired their art work. "That cookie looks good enough to eat," giggled Mrs. Gottfried clapping in approval. "Now, we better get you back to school." The boys piled into the car and arrived at the school in less than ten minutes.

Larry and Ray sprinted down the school hall when suddenly Larry dropped the poster on the way to the office. "Oy vey," cried out Ray picking up the poster. "Oy vey," repeated Larry as he picked up the poster, "It's okay, Ray, not even a scratch."

They tapped on Mr. Gillespie's door, and poked in their heads, "Thanks for everything," Larry called out.

"Hold on there boys, mind if I look at your new poster?" The Head Master smiled in approval. "Wait just a moment." He returned with a little step stool. "Hope you don't mind if I help you pin it up – **high** on the wall."

Done. Mission accomplished. The three of them stood back and admired the art work.

"When the election is over, I would like to keep this one in my office, if that's okay with you?" The Head Master's words were more of a statement than a question.

Both boys smiled and shook their heads, "Sure," in approval. Larry thought this poster looked even better than the first one. So far, so good. He turned to Ray for a high-five, when suddenly, Mr. Gillespie got between them, held up his hands and gave each of  them a firm high-five. "Good luck with the election tomorrow," he said returning to the office.

Larry wondered why Mr. Gillespie wanted to keep his poster. He never found out, but that poster stayed in the office during the four years Larry attended Edison High. For all Larry knew, it might be there to this day.

Chapter 13

Larry Runs for Office

Larry worked on his election speech all night. It was almost eleven o'clock when he turned off his lamp.

At the end of first period, the students filed into the auditorium to listen to the student speeches. The freshman offices were first. Larry and the other candidates sat on the stage waiting for the Head Master to address the entire school. Larry's hands felt cold and sweaty as he sat there. The lights blinded him. His knees felt weak. Then he remembered something his mother had told him. "Look out at the very last row and pretend your father and I are sitting there – proudly smiling at you. Then smile back at us," she had prompted him.

That's exactly what Larry did. Then something in the first row caught his attention. What was it? Who was it?

"Our first candidate this morning is Mr. Larry Chu," Mr. Gillespie was announcing him. It took Larry several seconds to realize he was being called up to the microphone. "Larry Chu? That's me," he said to himself. He swallowed hard, and jumped up to the microphone. Holding it tightly, Larry squinted to see who was in the front row that had distracted him. It was his two friends, Akemi and Ray. What was that in their hands? They were holding up a little sign with his name on it. He took a deep breath, looked out over the heads of 300 students, all the way to the back row.

"Good morning. My name is Larry Chu. I am running for the office of Freshman Class president of the best school in the entire Bay Area. What makes it the best? You – each and every one of you. Sure, we may look a little different, come from different backgrounds, but deep down we share something very important. We are all Edison High students. We give this school its good name." The words were coming fast and easy to him, rolling off his tongue without any hesitation. Larry continued, "I urge you to try your best this semester, make it even better than last year."

Larry was off and running. He was still smiling and clutching the mic when he started his closing remarks.

"Thank you. Now, I would like you to turn to the person sitting on your right and give them a high-five." The students giggled as they did what Larry asked.

"Please turn to the person on your left and give them a high-five too," he continued, then waited patiently for the students to calm down before he spoke. "Remember to vote for Larry Chu. And, remember, you are the ones who give

this school the reputation of being the best and friendliest school in the Bay Area. Thank you."

As Larry left the stage he thought he could hear his friends chanting, "Larr- ree."

"Larr-ree. Larr-ree."

At the end of the day, the election results were posted outside the Head Master's office. The high-five kid had won. After checking the results and seeing his name, Larry darted down the hall giving everyone he saw a high-five as he left the school, jumped on his bike and raced home. By the time he got in the front door, he was out of breath.

"Mom," he shouted, panting to catch his breath. "The election results are in and guess what? It was one of the first times a Chinese boy was elected president of the freshman class."

As he spoke, he paused to inhale the delicious smell of a hot pork bun waiting for him on the table. Now it was Mother's turn to speak.

"It's not so hard to imagine, son. I never had any doubts. Guess your high-five campaign might have had something to do with it. Son, I am so proud of you. I predict this is just the first of many accomplishments. Sit down dear, I have a special treat for you." She moved close to hug him, and decided against it at the last moment. Up came Mother's hands to give the new freshman class president a big high-five.

Mother was right this was the first of Larry's many accomplishments over the next four years. There was no way of knowing then, but one day, before leaving the sheltered halls of Edison High, Larry Chu would be captain of the soccer and basketball team, class president for three of his four years at Edison School, and selected to travel to Russia with the drama club during the summer of 1991. In Larry's last year, just like Akemi Watanabe, he was voted student body president of Edison High.

When it came time to think about his future and apply to college, Larry and his friend, Ray Gotfried, decided their first choice was Georgetown University in Washington, D.C. It was an extremely stressful time for all seniors playing the waiting game to find out which college had accepted them. The competition was fierce throughout the United States. Stress hit every senior as he or she applied for college and had to wait months to hear a reply.

Ray and Larry talked about how they would handle the special letter when it was delivered to them. Would they learn their fate by first ripping open the mysterious letter with one try, or hold the envelope up to the light and try to guess their fate? The suspense was overwhelming. Larry wondered if he would get in to the college of his first choice.

Each night Larry and Ray would discuss the matter on the phone. Their conversation was always the same:

"Hi Ray, have you heard yet?"

"Hi, Larry, no, just a bunch of junk mail about some schools I never knew existed. Maybe we'll hear tomorrow."

Tomorrow finally came.

Chapter 14
College Waiting Game

So far, not so good. None of Larry's friends had been accepted into any of the Ivy League Universities, except for Frank Peabody. He was Dr. Peabody's son. Frank never went to the dances or played basketball or soccer after school. Franklin got into Harvard. "Maybe I should have taken physics and spent more time in the library like Frank," Larry lamented.

"Naw, you did everything right. Stop second guessing yourself," returned Ray.

The letter from Georgetown University finally came. Larry and Ray had made a pack that they would open their letters at the same time. Larry's letter arrived the day before and he had to let it sit on the table and marinate in the sun. He had promised Ray not to open the envelope until they both received their mail. That way, one boy would not know before the other.

The line was busy when Larry tried to dial Ray. On the second try, Ray answered. "It came. It's here, in my sweaty little palms," Ray proudly exclaimed on the phone as if he was holding a microphone announcing news on the radio.

"Cut out the drama, Ray. Let's get it over with. I can't wait any longer. How about at the count of three we open the envelope at the same time."

"Right," Ray agreed. "At the count of three then. ONE TWO THREE."

There was a ripping and tearing and heavy breathing sounds coming from the phone. Then complete silence. Not a sound. Silence.

It didn't take long to read the only words that mattered: "We regret to inform you . . ."

Ray was the first to come back on the line. He was direct. His words like a basketball aimed for the basket, flew right into to the net with, "I didn't get in."

Larry replied, "Me either."

"Want to talk about it Larry?"

"Nope."

"Me, either."

"See you in school tomorrow. Bye."

"Bye."

Conversation over. Life over. The facts hurt. The boys didn't get into the school of their choice. A knocking at his door startled Larry.

"It's Mom, and I would like to come in." Mother opened Larry's bedroom door and she sat down on the chair next to Larry's bed. "I think I can tell by the look on your face that you are a little disappointed."

"I failed," Larry started the conversation. "Mom, I failed to get into Georgetown."

"You didn't fail at anything, Larry. There just wasn't space for you and hundreds of other students. Georgetown isn't the only good university. Let's see what tomorrow's mail brings."

There were a lot of frowns on the faces of seniors the next few days at school. Even the high-five signs seemed a little weak. Larry and Ray ate lunch without the usual conversation. Then Ray said something Larry didn't know. "Did I ever tell you my mother never got into the university she applied for?"

"How could that be, she's such a successful graphic artist," said Larry. "I see her work on local magazine covers."

"Mom went to a junior college that specialized in art design. She was so good that eventually she opened her own studio. You see, Larry, everyone doesn't have to go to an Ivy League university to be successful. Did your Father, did Chef Chu go to college? I suspect he didn't go to a college, and look at him...he is the most successful and accomplished

Chinese Chef in the entire Bay Area. That's probably why your parents were invited to the White House. So cheer up. Maybe there's a special acceptance, letter waiting for us today. Call me the minute you get home, even before you open your mail."

The boys gave one another a hearty high-five and parted company. After school, Larry's father was waiting for him. A letter was also waiting.

"Okay, Dad, what did I do wrong? You never come home this early unless, unless . . ."

"Son, your mother is worried about you and asked me to talk to you. So here I am. Your mother said you didn't get into Georgetown. But, that's not the only good college out there. Mom and I feel other values are very important like a person's fine character. I've always told you kids, I don't care what you become, as long as you are good citizens – caring people who always try your best. Look at your brother, Jon, he wants to be a movie director. Who knows where in the world that will lead! Now, is there anything you want to ask me about my life?"

Larry shook his head, no. He had heard most of his father's life stories many times. "Maybe there is one thing, Dad. You never let any of us work in the restaurant while we were going to school. Isn't it a family rule that the eldest son becomes manager of the family business? Isn't practical working experience better than anything I will learn in college? I'll never be as successful as you are, Dad." Larry put his head down on his father's chest.

"You will, son. You **will** succeed at whatever you do."

"How can you be so sure, Dad?" Larry asked sadly as he pulled back and looked directly into his father's eyes.

"Because, Larry," Father continued slowly with an air of certainty in the tone of his voice. "Because, my blood flows through your veins." He put his arm around Larry's back. "Let's go into dinner, son. I believe I smell the scent of your favorite steamed pork buns. Besides, I think your friend, Ray, is waiting for your phone call after dinner. He's already called three times." Larry's father took him by the arm and they walked into the kitchen together.

The family was waiting for them and Mother had a special dinner on the table.

"Sit next to me, Larry," requested Howard. "I want you to tell me another funny story."

Before dinner was finished, the phone rang for the fourth time. "I think I can guess who that is," said Mother.

Larry went to his room to take Ray's call in private. "Did you hear from UCLA?"

"Why do you think I've been calling you all night? So, at the count of three we open the letters. Agree?"

"Agree," replied Larry. "A letter has been sitting on my desk, waiting for me to open it." He let his fingers rip through the edge of the envelope. "One, two three."

Silence. No one spoke, but each could hear the sound of paper rustling in the phone. More silence, then outbursts of laughter. "What's so funny?" Larry asked.

"I'll give you three guesses," replied Ray.

"I only need one," said Larry. "You got into UCLA, right? Me too."

More waves of uncontrollable laughter.

"It's a great school Larry – all the Cal schools are hard to get into and we're in!"

Both boys were exhausted from the suspense, tension and stress that had mounted up. They couldn't control their laughter and finally ended the call with, "Congratulations" and "Mazel Tov – UCLA, here we come."

Later that night, Mother knocked on Larry's door. "Can I come in and say good-night, Larry. I heard all this laughter. I want to know what's so funny?" she asked. Then, Mother sat down at the foot of Larry's bed.

"Larry," she sighed. "So far, things have often worked out for you. But the reality of life is, things don't always work out the way we want. I'm sorry you didn't get your first choice, but maybe . . ."

"It's okay, Mom," Larry yawned. Ray and I both got into UCLA."

"That's great son. Great. You see, it's possible that good things happen when you have patience to wait. We're so proud of you. I would like to see the letter." It was too late, Larry had drifted off to sleep with his clothes still on, and the acceptance letter clutched in his hand. Mother would have to wait until tomorrow to read the letter. She kissed her son on the forehead and turned off the light.

AUTHOR'S NOTE:

Several years later Mr. Gillespie, the Head Master, retired. Chef Chu and Mrs. Chu hosted a grand retirement party for him. At that occasion, Mr. Gillespie took the opportunity to take Larry and his mother aside to share some thoughts: "I will never forget Larry's graduation." He continued, "After the ceremony, everyone walked off and I was left to pick up all the chairs. I remember your kindness when all five youngsters in your family came to my rescue and helped fold the chairs and put them away."

Larry also shared some thoughts with Mr. Gillespie that night, "I will never forget your help with the poster I made when I was running for class office. Mr. Gillespie turned to give Larry a high-five.

"Good-luck at UCLA. Good luck my boy," he said to Larry. Then Mr. Gillespie turned to Chef Chu and Mrs. Chu and shook their hands in appreciation. "This is the greatest retirement party I could have ever imagined. Thank you so very much."

That was the last time Larry ever saw the Head Master.

Chapter 15

A Phone Call That Changed Lives

Larry had an effervescent personality, and made friends easily. He and Ray had their minds set on joining a certain fraternity their first year. However, neither one was chosen to be a potential member to join the fraternity of his choice.

Larry thought of his father's words when he felt the sting of disappointment. This was one of the times Father's advice helped him get over the hurdle of what Larry tried not to think of as a rejection. Chef Chu had said to his son, "Larry, *don't let success go to your head, or what you consider as a failure—go to your heart.*"

Both boys were accepted into the fraternity of their choice, their second year at the University. Even though in different fraternities, the two remained close friends.

There were times during those years in college when Larry thought of his mother's advice also. Her words of wisdom went something like this: *"Remember to do your best. Things don't always work out the way we want. We have to learn to adjust and make good decisions."*

Larry would be called on to make the hardest adjustment in his life. It happened a few weeks before Spring break, his third year at the university. Larry got a phone call from Mother. It started off like most of the other calls from home. "Hey, Mom, what's up? What's new with Dad? How's Howard doing?"

"Howard is fine. Jon and Jennifer are trying to pitch in and take over where you left off. I hope you are eating well son. Is there something besides salami sandwiches in your refrigerator?" Mother asked.

"So far, so good, Mom. Of course, nothing can compare to your cooking."

"Any girlfriends? How are your grades?"

"No serious girlfriends at this point. Ray joined another fraternity and we decided to rent an apartment with another friend instead of living at the fraternity next semester. Grades? Yep, they are fine and I am still an Economics Major. Enough about me, do you and Dad have any special Easter plans? How's your golf game coming along?"

Then Mother came out with words Larry never dreamed he would hear her say.

Mother interrupted Larry, "I'm calling for another reason. I want to tell you something."

"Okay. Something about the family? Anything wrong, Mom?"

"They found a lump in my breast. I was just diagnosed with cancer," she came right out with it.

"Cancer?" Larry wasn't sure he had heard her correctly. He repeated what he thought she had said, "Did you say cancer, Mom?"

"Yes, son, they found a lump in my breast. The doctor said I will need radiation and chemotherapy."

"Slow down a minute, Mom. I'm not getting all this."

Words were being said that Larry didn't understand, words like: cancer, chemotherapy, radiation . . . "

"You are just telling me this now? How long have you known? Mom, are you okay?"

Larry was only twenty years old at the time, and a junior in college. The word "cancer" didn't register with him. Larry could hear Mother's voice, but he was not understanding the new words she used. Cancer? What did that have to do with his mother?

"Mom, are you going to be okay? When does your treatment start? I'm coming right home to be there for you. I'll call to make a plane reservation as soon as I hang up."

No reply. There was an ominous silence on the phone. For a moment it seemed they had been disconnected. "Mom,

Mom, are you still there?" Silence. The news struck Larry like a lightning bolt from out of the blue.

"Larry, I have to rest more these days."

"What?"

Larry reacted spontaneously without waiting for a further explanation, "Look, Mom, I'm taking the next plane home."

"No. No. Larry," Mother said forcefully. "You have final exams coming up. You have to stay right there."

"Do you think I can concentrate on finals after what you just told me? Look, Mom, under the circumstances, I can get permission to take my exams at a later date. Besides, you always told me life was taking one step at a time, and I'm taking that first step right now. Tell Dad I will be on the first morning flight back the day after tomorrow. Rest up, Mom, I'll be there soon."

Larry discussed the situation with his professors, and got permission to take the exams after he returned from home. He packed a few of his books and clothes in a suitcase and got an early flight out two days later.

His Father was waiting for him in the car when Larry arrived at San Jose Mineta International Airport. After a few brief words, the two drove the 25 minutes back to their Los Altos home in silence.

When they arrived home, Mother was resting in bed. She looked the same as usual, except for the fact his mother would never still be in bed this late in the morning, and she looked a little pale. She reached out to hold her son's hand, held it tighter than usual and smiled. The two spoke no words, but their eyes relayed a message that only they could understand.

"I'll make you some hot tea, Mom." With that, he placed her hand gently down on the bed and left the room.

The family surrounded Larry once he closed the bedroom door and left Mother's room. Everyone began talking at once. They seemed to have more questions than answers.

Father was the first to speak. "Aunt Lois has been here and brought food for the family. The neighbors have been wonderful. The doctor has outlined the treatment saying she will need several rounds of chemotherapy and perhaps some radiation. The good news is . . . the doctor says Mom's outlook looks favorable. I am thinking of hiring someone to stay with Mom so I can get back to the restaurant."

"No need to get anyone, Dad. I'm here now. I'm the oldest, and the best one to take care of Mom. Besides, I'm not going back to college so soon. Summer is almost here anyway and I have permission from my professors to take the exams once I return."

There was very little discussion – it was agreed, Larry would be home for the next few months to help his mother get through the ordeal that she was about to face.

His first task was to bring Mother some warm tea. A fond memory flashed into his thoughts of the many times his mother had brought him a warm pork bun to lighten his mood. It had worked. He warmed up a big pork bun, put it on a fancy plate and brought it into her bedroom. Finding her asleep, he left the plate on her nightstand so that whenever she awoke, it would be waiting for her. The warm scent woke his mother up for a moment. She smiled, then fell back asleep.

Howard, his younger brother, was waiting for Larry when he returned from the bedroom. His next task was to keep Howard calm and try to explain, in a way his autistic brother would understand, that his mother needed lots of rest, and that the medicine she was taking would make her well.

"Mom is sick, Howie," he began.

"Want to see Mom," Howard took Larry's arm and shook it hard as if he expected an answer to come from his brother's arm. "Is she very, very sick? Tell me, Larry," he pleaded.

"Yes, Howard, Mom is very sick that's why I came home to help. But, I want you to know the medicine and rest will help her get well. Mom is sleeping right now, Howard. I have come home to help her get well."

"How about me? I want to help too," replied his brother. "I want to help Mom get well."

Larry thought long and hard about what he would say next. Then, he turned to Howard, took his arm away from his brother's strong grip and replied, "I know a way you can help." Slowly and carefully, Larry thought about each word before he started talking to Howard. They had to be the right words – words Howard would understand. "Yes. I have an idea that is perfect for you to make Mom feel better. You can be Mom's pillow man."

"Pillow man?" asked Howard. "What's a pillow man, Larry? I want to help Mom get well." Pillow man sounded very important to Howard. "What's a pillow man?"

"It's a very important job, and it's just for you," replied Larry.

"Important job," repeated Howard joyfully.

The idea started to take shape in Larry's thoughts. He had his answer and he thought it would work. In the morning he would set his plan into motion.

Howard was up earlier than usual and met Larry outside Mother's bedroom door. She was already dressed and ready to leave for her third chemotherapy infusion. Larry had breakfast waiting for her. While Mother ate, Larry and Howard entered the bedroom to make her bed. He noticed the pork bun had barely been eaten. The sheets and blankets were strewn all around the bed and on the floor. Larry picked them up and made the bed. Then he turned to Howard and outlined the "pillow man training."

"See how crumbled this pillow is," he held up the pillow. "Does this look like a comfortable pillow? No."

"No," Howard repeated. "Make the pillow good, Larry."

"Would you want to sleep on this pillow Howie? Of course not." Larry answered his own question and continued, "I will show you how to make the pillow comfortable for Mother."

"Pillow not good, Larry. Fix it for Mom," Howard insisted.

"Okay. Now watch carefully. Are you watching Howie?"

"Watching," came the reply.

"So, first I shake the pillow like this." Larry shook the pillow forcefully.

"Next, I put the pillow back on the bed and smack it with my open hand. Watch me, Howie." Larry pounded the pillow and got out all the bumps. "Next, I smooth out the pillow and stand back to see how comfortable it looks. Did you get all that? Now, Pillow Man, it's your turn."

"Howie wants to be Mom's pillow man."

"Good," said Larry handing Howard the other messed up pillow. Larry repeated the steps slowly, praising his brother as each step was mastered. Then, they repeated the procedure together again. Finally, Mother's two pillows lay side by side on a perfectly made bed.

"Want to test pillow out. Want to make sure it is good enough for Mom. Pillow man did a good job," Howard said proudly.

"Good job," repeated Larry giving his little brother a high-five.

With that, Howard put his head down on Mother's pillow and closed his eyes.

Chapter 16

Cancer Treatment Begins

With a heavy heart Larry drove his mother to the Treatment Center. Trying to muster up an air of confidence, he held her arm as they entered the waiting room. Mother seemed in good spirits, but Larry wasn't sure if it was an act for his benefit.

There were five other patients sitting in the waiting room when they arrived. It was a pleasant room decorated with flowers and pictures. A nurse was at the front desk waiting to register Mrs. Chu. Then the two were told to take a seat and that there would only be a short waiting period.

"Everything's going to be okay, Mom. I'm here to take care of you."

"I know, son," Mother replied. "You have always been the one I could count on."

The first lady was called. She appeared to be older than Larry's mother. She wore a bright colored hat that sat low on her head. Her face seemed a little puffy. Larry couldn't imagine his mother ever looking like that.

"See if you can find a good magazine to read while you are waiting for me." Mother pointed to a table where an array of magazines were neatly displayed.

"Mrs. Chu. Mrs. Ruth Chu." The nurse's voice sent a chill through Larry. It was like the feeling he had in the pit of his stomach when his teacher called out his name to recite a phrase of poetry and he wasn't prepared. But it wasn't his name being called. The nurse was calling his mother's name. She called it again. This time Mother got up. As the nurse was taking Larry's mother into another room, she paused to speak to him. "If you want, you can come in with your mother and keep her company while she has her treatment today."

Mother stopped Larry just as he was getting up. "Not this time, dear," she said.

"This will take approximately two hours," the nurse announced. "Can I get you water or some juice while you wait for your mother?"

"No, thank you," he told the nurse. Then he turned to his mother. "I will be waiting right here for you. Oh, I almost forgot the snack," Larry said taking out a small bag from his backpack. "Dad prepared a little snack for you." He handed the paper bag to his mother. "Thanks," she replied letting a wide grin sweep across her face as she followed the nurse into another room. Then she was gone.

From the moment the door closed behind his mother, Larry suddenly felt alone. But he wasn't alone, there were still four other patients in the room. All waiting, waiting for their names to be called.

Larry tried to pass the time by picking a magazine to read. He flipped through the pages, looking at the pictures. He couldn't seem to concentrate on the words.

Time seemed to pass slowly. "Mrs. Whitley." Someone's name was being called. A woman got up to meet the nurse. They exchanged pleasant greetings, then she was escorted into the treatment room. Now there were three patients left. He tried not to stare at them.

Larry got up and explored the posters that were on the walls. Some of them told of cancer support groups. He checked one out that listed special resources and classes. He returned to his seat and the magazine and pretended to read, but he couldn't concentrate. All Larry could think of was wondering what was on the other side of the door where his mother was getting a treatment that would help her win the fight with this thing called cancer.

After about two hours, the door opened and the nurse brought out his mother. Larry jumped up to greet her. It was as though she had been away for the whole day.

"Would you like a wheel chair to the car, Mrs. Chu?" the nurse asked.

"No, thank you. I'm fine. My son is here."

Larry took his mother's arm and the two walked slowly to the car, which Larry had parked right in front of the office.

"Do you want to talk about it, Mom?"

"I feel fine, Larry. There was no pain involved. They just put the medicine into my body through a little needle inserted into my arm. There were other people in the room getting the same treatment. One lady was about my age. The two of us talked, and the time seemed to pass quickly. She knew all about our restaurant and told me about the time her family celebrated birthdays with their six children at Chef Chu's."

Mother continued, "It wasn't bad at all. I ate the snack Dad prepared for me, and the time passed quickly. The nurse explained that I probably will be tired and maybe I won't be able to eat everything, but she gave me pills for all that. There seems to be a pill for everything. I have a list of foods to eat and medicine to take."

"I want to go in with you next time, Mom, and keep you company. Maybe we can play cards or something. Sorry, Mom, I just remembered you don't play cards."

"We'll see," Mother smiled and repeated, "We'll see."

When they got home, Mother had a little rice soup Father had waiting for her. After eating it, she went right to bed.

The next morning, when the children came in to greet her, Mother said she had slept fine. "You must have bought me a new pillow. It was so comfortable." Mother winked at Larry. Larry in turn winked at Howard and then gave him a high-five hand sign.

The treatment lasted for five weeks. Mother lost her hair and didn't have much of an appetite. She slept more than usual, but in the end, the doctor told them they had caught the cancer in time. After a few months passed, Mother's hair started growing again. Eventually, she regained her energy and joined her friends playing golf. When Larry noticed she was feisty as ever, he felt reassured – at last, he knew his mother was back.

So far, so good. It was time for him to return to UCLA.

Chapter 17

The Typhoon of 1996

After college graduation Larry and Ray took an extended trip touring China. Larry loved Hong Kong and had mixed feelings about leaving.

Then, the unexpected happened.

It was called Typhoon Sally.

The public had been warned the typhoon would be severe. The boys were told this storm would punch a blow like they had never experienced in California. Ray decided to return home to a job that was waiting for him. Now Larry had to make a decision before his plane tickets expired.

On that day in late August, there were few people on the streets that were usually crowded at this time. The bright explosion from the crackling lightning, embellished by the sound of thunder, caused people to run for shelter, but not Larry. He had one goal in mind . . . to get to the ticket office.

Thick sheets of heavy rain, pushed by the raging wind, slanted down on the city. Larry had on a thin, translucent rain poncho, not appropriate for this weather. The rain saturated his slacks and plastered down his hair. He took his

hand to mop his forehead and push the hair away from his eyes. It was still difficult to see. The wind was so intense, it was hard to walk straight. He was within one block of the airline office, but the intensity of the wind made it seem like a mile away. The wind whipped around him – howling, hissing, and holding him back.

Suddenly, with the last clash of thunder, a scene from his grandmother's funeral flashed in front of him. It happened long ago when he was 13, and his dearest *Boo-Boo* (Chinese for grandmother) was laid to rest at the cemetery. It was a stormy day such as today. Was *Boo-Boo* trying to send him a message?

The vision was gone as soon as he jumped out of the way to dodge a low-flying branch from a near-by tree.

Now, the crackling lightning and sound of thunder seemed right overhead. It was becoming more difficult for Larry to catch his breath. At last, Larry was in front of the airline office door. He pounded on the glass window pane with the palms of his wet, clammy hands. Inside the office, Larry could see the lights flicking off and on. Someone was coming toward the door. A tall, slender woman attempted to open the door, but the wind was no match for her strength. She called for help. Finally, with the assistance of two people, the door was opened wide enough to let Larry in and push the howling wind back. Then the door slammed shut with great force.

"What in the world are you doing out in this storm, young man?" the airline employee asked. Without answering, Larry made his way to the ticket window and pulled out his limp ticket.

"I need to make an exchange," he said with a tone of doubt in his voice. A very wet, soggy, young man stood in front of the airline employee deep in thought. In his head, Larry kept hearing his mother's words, "Come right home, or I'm coming there to get you."

Should he postpone his flight or cancel it? His dad had reminded him, that although he hadn't started the job yet, he had made a commitment to work at a company in San Francisco. Ray had already left ahead of the typhoon, and accepted a position in New York. There was no one with whom he could talk, no one to discuss the pros and cons of his decision. The choice he would make today, could very likely have an impact on the rest of his life.

"Well, young man," the airline agent waited patiently for an answer. "We are closing early today due to the typhoon. This is just the beginning of it, you know. Now, what can we do for you before we have to close the office?"

Larry loved Hong Kong. Should he stay or should he go home? This was a decision he would have to live with, and he had to make it alone.

What was he going to do?

The impatient employee continued, "Do you want to postpone your flight until next week? Next month?"

No reply. Then suddenly, out it came, "Next year," Larry proclaimed. "One year from today, please. 1997."

A new ticket was printed out and Larry placed it in his shirt pocket that was dry.

"Thank you," he called back as the two employees helped push him out the door against the wind's force that had diminished in intensity.

Once outside, Larry noticed the rain had stopped. The air was still. Larry took in a deep breath. He thought about his beloved grandmother again. It was just like the weather on the day of *Boo-Boo's* funeral. After she was put to rest, the sun came out and all was calm again. He could always talk to *Boo-Boo* when he was troubled and looked for a solution. Today, he had made a decision that would affect the rest of his life.

A few people started coming back outside. For the moment, there was no wind to fight as he walked back to the youth hostel where he was temporarily staying. He felt like a kid again sloshing through some puddles allowing a little water to enter his shoes. He belonged here. He felt complete. At the moment, he felt accepted, at peace with himself.

Larry paused to see reflections of the tall buildings wavering in the rain soaked sidewalk. It was as if the city was calling to him, "Welcome home, Larry Chu. Welcome to Hong Kong."

Chapter 18
Living in Hong Kong

Worrying about his future, Larry walked slowly back to the youth hostel, deep in thought. He had made the decision to remain in Hong Kong, the land of his father's birth. He hoped it was the right decision.

Larry knew he couldn't stay at the youth hostel much longer. He would have to find an apartment and a job. He had spent two weeks looking and so far, no luck. He had no place to go. No job. No prospects. As reality set in, he felt his stomach do somersaults. It was then that he remembered his mother's words, "We have to work with the cards we are dealt." Even though he knew his mother never played cards, those words made sense to him. Somehow, thinking about her, put him in a positive frame of mind.

Once he was back in his room at the youth hostel, Larry threw his clothes in a heap on the floor and stepped into a hot shower. The warm water made him feel better and helped clear his head. He got dressed and noticed the new plane ticket had fallen out of his shirt pocket. He turned it over in his hands and then stuffed it carefully back in his wallet.

Larry tried to piece events of the past week together and make sense of all that had happened. His thoughts were broken up by a message he received telling him he had a phone call.

The message was from Romo, the person he and Ray had hiked with in the mountains above Hong Kong. Quickly, he dialed the phone number. The phone rang three times. "Come on Romo, pick up the phone. Be home," he mumbled to himself, "Be home." On the fourth ring someone answered the phone.

"Hello."

"Hello, Romo, is that you? This is Larry. Gee, it's good to hear your voice. Got a message that you called."

"Larry, so glad you returned my call. I remember what a good time the three of us had hiking, and I thought you might have decided to return home after the typhoon. I figure you have to leave the hostel soon, and I wanted to talk to you before you left. Say, have you found an apartment yet?"

"No. I've been looking, but so far no luck."

"Well, Larry, your luck has just changed," said Romo.

"What do you mean? What's up?" Larry inquired.

"I've got to go on a business trip for at least one month. If things work out in my favor, it may even be longer. So, do you want to rent my apartment until I return? I know this is short notice, but . . . you really would be doing me a favor."

"Thanks for the offer, and yes. Yes. I'm ready to move in tomorrow. Just say the word."

"The word is *today.* Today is a lucky day for both of us. Can you be ready to move in on short notice, like tomorrow?"

"Tomorrow can't come soon enough, Romo. I'll be there first thing in the morning. And, Romo, thanks again for the offer."

The next day Larry took his few things, stuffed them into his backpack and arrived at Romo's apartment by 10 a.m. in the morning. The two young men exchanged a high-five greeting and sat down to talk in Romo's small living room.

"Nice apartment," said Larry as he made a quick look around.

"It's small, but location is the main thing. We are close to the center of town," replied Romo.

The apartment was small, but furnished tastefully. Larry went to the front room window to check out the view, when Romo called him back and asked him to sit down. Romo gave him some good job leads and then gave Larry phone numbers of some of his personal friends to contact.

"I think Susanna would be a good contact for you," he said. "She has lived here all her life and the two of you have lots in common. Her parents own a restaurant business, just like yours. And besides she's a great person. Any questions, Larry? If not, here are the keys, I hope you don't mind my leaving this quickly, but I have a plane to catch."

That was that. Larry's luck had changed as quickly as Romo dashed out of the apartment. As some of his friends back home would say, "So far, so good."

Larry didn't waste any time. After he said goodbye and wished his friend good luck, he settled into his new apartment. Before dinner time, he had already called several of the phone numbers Romo left for him. He lined up two job interviews and called to introduce himself to Susanna.

Larry was starting to feel at home in his new dwelling. He had no doubts now that his decision to remain in Hong Kong was the right one. One of the job interviews culminated in an offer to work in the marketing offices of a large company. He saw Susanna frequently and enjoyed visiting with her parents. They had a chance to discuss issues that were prevalent in both countries. The couple soon discovered how much they had in common, and a wonderful friendship developed.

Romo returned from his trip, and asked Larry to stay on as his roommate. Now, Larry's problem of finding another place to stay was solved. Things started to fall in place and Larry was content and happy. The next two years passed quickly. It appeared to Larry that he had found a new place to call "home." Then, one day, an invitation arrived in the mail announcing the graduation of Jonathan Chu. His brother was graduating from the University of Southern California (USC), and it was time for Larry to return home and participate in the big family celebration. He wasted no time getting his ticket, and made plans to fly back.

Larry's father picked him up at the airport and didn't stop asking questions until they arrived back at the hotel where the family was staying. It felt good to be back and see how great his mother looked. Larry had a good feeling about spending time with everyone, but in his heart he knew China was the place where he belonged now, and he was anxious to tell everyone about Susanna and his new life in Hong Kong.

After the graduation ceremony, Larry was just about to take a walk around the campus to bask in the warm, California sunshine. Then, his father grabbed his arm, and took him aside. "I need to have a private talk with you, son," he said. There was a serious look on his face, almost as serious as the time Mother's cancer was discovered.

"Son," Father tapped his fingers on the table to get Larry's attention. "There is something extremely important I have to ask you."

112

Chapter 19

Howie Has the Last Word

Father got right to the point. "Son," he began, "I have to know if you are interested in the family business. I am making long range plans for the restaurant – next year, five years from now, 15, 20 and so on."

For a brief moment, Larry hesitated. He was at a loss for words, and he had to have the right words. Father was waiting, and he wanted an answer now.

"Dad," he began, choosing his words cautiously. "There are many things for me to consider. I love living in Hong Kong, I have a job now, and there is Susanna – who I really think is the right person for me. Dad, I have to think carefully about my answer."

"Sure. Sure. Of course, son. How about tonight, when we get back home. Will you have an answer for me tonight?"

"How about tomorrow? We will celebrate Jonathan's graduation at a special family dinner tomorrow," replied Larry.

"Yes, yes. Tomorrow is fine," Dad replied. "Take all the time you need. Tomorrow is fine."

All the way home, the short hour flight from Los Angeles to San Francisco airport, Larry was deep in thought considering his future. Father was quiet also. He was considering the future of Chef Chu's Restaurant. What would the future hold for father and son? It was another decision Larry had to make alone – one that would affect the rest of his life and Susanna's life. It had to be the right decision.

Once they were home, Larry's sisters got busy helping Mother with dinner preparations. The kitchen was filled with wonderful smells of favorite dishes. Larry took time to check out his bedroom, let his fingers test a few of the ivory keys on the family's out-of-tune piano, and stop to talk to Howie before they gathered for dinner.

Howie sat down next to Larry at the dinner table. It was then Larry noticed the solemn look on Father's face. When dinner was served, Father barely touched his food. Everyone, was happy and busy talking, asking Jonathan and Larry questions. Father was silent. He remained deep in his own thoughts. It was not like him to be so quiet, especially at a family celebration. Finally, Father made a move. He turned to look at Larry who sat directly across from him.

"Well, Larry, do you have an answer for me?" he asked.

A hush fell over the kitchen table. The air seemed heavy with anticipation. All eyes turned to look at Father, then at

Larry. For a brief moment there was silence. Larry thought it seemed as though they were all holding their breath waiting for someone to speak.

Larry was the first to speak. "Yes, Dad. I do have an answer for you. Two words." He swallowed hard to get the words out. **"I'm in,"** came the loud reply. The family's tension was relieved in a collective sigh. Suddenly all was right again. Father got up and started serving everyone more food. He danced around the back of their chairs calling out, *"Chi-fan. Chi-fan.* Eat everyone. Eat. We have much to celebrate tonight."

Larry thought the last time he saw Father this animated and excited was when the invitation from the White House arrived. Father ran from one person to the next calling, *"Chi-fan. Chi-fan* everyone. Mother has made a wonderful dinner. This is a celebration."

"Luta," Father called out enthusiastically. "Luta bring out the pork buns. This is a celebration. More pork buns for everyone, Luta."

Father didn't realize it, but Mother was already serving the pork buns.

"Luta, pork buns for the celebration," Father called out louder.

"Yes, Lawrence, a very good idea," said Mother as she winked at Larry.

Sensing the joy that permeated in the room that evening, Howie sang out, "Celebration. More pork buns for all please!" With those words, Howie got out of his seat, threw up both hands and reached down to give Larry a firm high-five.

Suddenly, in a spontaneous moment, each family member turned to the next person, and the joy of extending the high-five went around the room involving everyone and stopping where it had all started, with Howie.

Chef Chu's Restaurant
1067 N. San Antonio Rd., Los Altos

Established February 2, 1970, Chef Chu's restaurant celebrated 50 years in 2020. At that time, they have served over two million customers. Larry Chu is now General Manager and partner.

Chef Chu's
Lawrence C.C. Chu
Steamed Pork Buns

Prepared bread dough is shaped into buns and then filled with a stuffing made of diced barbecued pork, green onion, and flavorful oyster sauce. When steamed, they become puffy and white. Pork buns are prepared all over China though they originated in Canton province.

Makes: 12 to 18 snacks

Cooking time: 25 minutes

1 recipe Basic Bread Dough

1 tablespoon vegetable oil

FILLING

1/2 Pound Chinese Barbecued Pork, diced

1 green onion (white part minced

1/2 cup chicken broth

3 tablespoons oyster sauce

1 tablespoon dry sherry

1 tablespoon sugar

1/4 teaspoon salt

   Cornstarch paste

1/2 teaspoon sesame oil

Prepare dough as directed in Basic Bread Dough recipe.

To stir-fry, heat wok (or wide frying pan) over high heat for 1 minute until hot. Add oil and swirl pan to coat sides. When oil is hot, add pork and onion, stirring for 30 seconds. Mix in broth, oyster sauce, sherry, sugar, and salt. Bring to a boil, thicken with 1 tablespoon cornstarch paste and sprinkle with sesame oil. Transfer to a bowl , cool, and refrigerate until thickened.

To assemble, roll dough into a cylinder about 2 inches in diameter. Cut cylinder into pieces 1 1/2 inches wide. With a cut side up, press down with palm of hand to flatten. Place 1 tablespoon filling in center of dough. Gather up edges of dough around filling in loose folds. Bring folds together at top and twist securely to make a stem.

To steam, line the inside of a bamboo steamer with we cheesecloth. Arrange buns on cheesecloth, cover, and steam over boiling water for 12 minutes.

Basic Bread Dough

What a rich chicken broth is to a soup, this basic bread dough is to many of my Chinese pastries or snacks. You're lost without it! Even in China, a cooks's all-purpose steamed bread dough is the basis for any type of dumpling, cake, or bun.

Makes: 1 recipe dough

Cooking time: None

3/4 cup warm water (about 110°F)

1 tablespoon sugar

1/2 cup warm mild (about 110°F)

1/2 package active dry yeast

4 cups all-purpose flour

1/2 teaspoon baking powder

Combine water and sugar well. Stir in milk and check temperature (it should be about 110°F) Add yeast, stirring to dissolve, and set aside until mixture begins to bubble. Gradually add flour, mixing as you go. Knead for 3 to 4 minutes and shape into a ball and cover with a damp cloth to rise in a warm, draft-free spot for about 1 hour or until double in size.

Turn dough out onto a floured board, flatten slightly and sprinkle surface with baking powder. Knead for about 5 minutes until smooth. Set aside, covered, until ready to use.

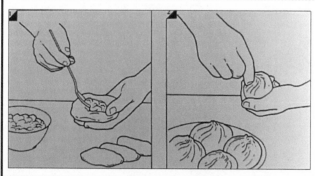

Place 1 tablespoon filling in center of flattened dough. Gather up edges around filling in loose folds. Bring together at top and twist securely to seal and make a small stem.

Thank you to, Chef Chu, for granting permission to reprint his recipes from his cookbook, *Celebrating Your Place at Our Table*, available to purchase on Amazon.com.

119

Chef, Lawrence Chu and Family
1983
Left to right: Larry Jr., Mrs. Ruth Chu, holding
Jonathan, Chef Chu, holding Howard, Jennifer,
and Chrissy

Mrs. Ruth Chu, son,
Larry and daughter
Chrissy. 1976

Top and left photos:
Larry Chu Jr., wife, Susanna and their son, Larry.

Bottom Photo
Larry Chu Jr., his parents, Mr. and Mrs. Lawrence Chu, and sister, Chrissy

About the Author

Norma Slavit, a former Master Teacher, taught in the elementary schools of New Rochelle, New York and San Francisco. She also taught music at Hillbrook, a private school in Los Gatos, California.

The author was a newspaper editor for the JCC Community Center in Palo Alto for 13 years. Slavit's articles and stories have appeared in educational journals, magazines and newspapers. She has one published play to her credit, and an early story appeared in the Encyclopedia Britannica reading series.

Slavit is a member of SCBWI as well as the National League of American Pen Women. Her first book, *Peaches, Frog and the Man in the Moon* is a picture book for children four to eight years old. *The Elephant Who Had Allergies* is for children of all ages. *September Thanksgiving* is a chapter book for the middle grades. *Pork Buns and High-Fives* is a chapter book for middle school children, and is based on the memoirs of an Asian boy growing up in Silicon Valley. All of Norma's books contain an educational component for teacher and parent.

About the Illustrator

Judith (Jude) Tolley grew up in Virginia, and spent a great deal of time in the Washington, D.C. museums. She attended Virginia Commonwealth University in Richmond, Virginia, graduating with a degree in Painting and Printmaking. She furthered her studies by attending classes at the National Academy of Design in New York City, and apprenticed with painters, Dani Dawson and Nelson Shanks. Additionally, she studied sculpture with Bruno Lucchesi.

Always fascinated with how things move, energy in motion, Tolley worked for many years in the animation industry, including at Walt Disney Feature Animation. Tolley received grants from the D.C. Commission on the Arts, in Washington, D.C., to introduce art programs into several D.C. schools. Students from seven schools produced animated films which were shown on WETA-TV (PBS) in two specials entitled, *A Capital Kids' Celebration of Animation* and *A Capital Kids' Celebration of Animation II.* Currently, Tolley maintains a studio near San Jose, California, and has won several awards in juried art shows for her paintings.